William Tarrant

Ningpo to Shanghai in 1857

William Tarrant

Ningpo to Shanghai in 1857

ISBN/EAN: 9783337342999

Printed in Europe, USA, Canada, Australia, Japan

Cover: Foto ©Andreas Hilbeck / pixelio.de

More available books at **www.hansebooks.com**

NINGPO

TO

SHANGHAI

IN 1857.

[VIA THE BORDERS OF AN-WHUI PROVINCE, HOO-CHOW-FOO AND THE GRAND CANAL.]

CANTON:

PRINTED AT THE "FRIEND OF CHINA" OFFICE.

1862

PREFACE,

The following pages were printed off as they were written, shortly after the writer's return to Hongkong in 1857, and would have been published before, had time allowed the preparation of a map and index which he intended to accompany the itinerary,

Almost the whole of the country travelled over has since fallen into the hands of the rebels, so that, though late, what is now submitted will prove useful to future travellers in affording materials for a contrast.

WILLIAM TARRANT,

Canton, January 21st, 1862,

INDEX TO ORDER OF TRAVEL.

U-TSIEN DISTRICT.

DEPARTMENT OF NINGPO.

District of Ningpo.

KONG KEAO 江 口 (Stream's mouth) is a small village of one street on the right bank of a wide stream, crossed, though fordable in the dry season, by a substantial roofed bridge. This bridge is lined on the village or southern side, for about a hundred feet, with small shops and idol depositaries.

Proceeding from KONG-KEAO to NING-KONG JOW * the course, to the right of a seven storied Pagoda on the hill over the north bank of the stream, is about N. by W. the distance 14 miles. The road, or pathway, about five feet wide, is laid with round and rough dark red granite blocks. Road ways of similar description, in some cases improved with a centre line of flat slabs, are found to run between most of the villages and thorough-fares throughout the province (Chekiang);—stone tablets here and there bearing and immortalizing the names of the individuals by whose means the works were effected.

The most unpleasant part of the travelling in this quarter is the continued sight of and effluvia from ordure pans and necessaries on the sides of the road. In half a dozen hours' travelling, as many as half a hundred of these necessaries are to be seen, and of pans;

---

* The Chinese characters for this as well as the names of the other places mentioned will be found in a separate index.

about three feet across and of similar depth, the number is uncountable. 'I he absence of other material for manure is, of course, the apology ; though, as such things are not met with in such profusion, or in *such display* in other parts of the province, the apology is a poor one. The land yields two crops annually--that of the autumn will be rice principally ;—of the spring, Wheat, Grassicher (1) Beans, Tea and Clover. The latter is grown over the Paddy stumps, with which it is afterwards ploughed up and left to rot and enrich the soil. The Teas, Beans, and Bean seed of the Grassicher spoken of, are cultivated principally for the oil expressed from them. The leaves and sprouts of the latter are eaten as a vegetable. The region hereabout, however, is remarkable for the production of a medicinal bulb called ряоумяо 貝 母 (2) Growing as a grass, its blades resemble those of the carnation. It is planted in the fourth month of one year and remins until the fourth month of the year following, when it is taken up and sold to Druggets as a tonic for sixty cash a catty. During the year of its growth, Potatoes, Hemp or Cotton may be grown over it. A mow of land produces from two to five hundred Ching (3) of the bulb in a year. Rushes for mat making are grown here too, and Mulberry und Tallow trees flourish largely. From the berry of the latter the candles used in Chekiang are made. Coated with animal fat they burn well, though the clumsy bamboo wicks, swathed with cotton twist, emit a good deal of unpleasant smoke.

To reach *Ning Kong jow,* the stream has to be crossed three times, one of the bridges at a place called *Seang-koh deo,* with some 3,500 inhabitants, being rooofed over as at *Kong Keo.* About 5 *lé* (4) from *Seang'ko deo* is another village called *Dung-jehow* with 100 families ; — a family being estimated as consisting on the average of five souls. There may be other causes apart from the prac-

tice of recording families in the ancestral hall which
induce an acquaintance with the subject ;—but it is
a circumstance of note that a Chinese, however low
his rank, if asked the number of families in his village is invariably prompt with a reply,—and in
three answers out of four the number approximates.

As *Ning kong jow* is often visited by Missionaries from Ningpo, no more need be said of it
than that it appears to be a place of considerable
traffic in timber and bamboos, as seen in rafts on
the stream. Of its reported 3 000 families it boasts
a fine ancestral Hall of the 富 *Foo* family.

Four *lé* from *Ning kong jow*, in a Sou' westerly
direction, is a village called *Pow she hoe* The
scenery on the road is most pleasing; the high
cliffs overhanging the stream giving it the character of the country about the Swiss Lakes. Fishing
with cormorants is common here;—the house
wives busy with cotton spinning.

About three miles from *Pow she ho* in a Nor' westerly direction is the *Heaven Struck rock*, a
spot of considerable note among the natives of
the district. The path way to it is cut out of
solid brown lava like rock,—the hill angling up at
about 80° to a height of seven or eight hundred feet.
Teen tung gun is the native name of the locality.
The stream at this place, though shallow, flows
rapidly from the Eastward.

A little to the northward of *Teen tung gun*
is the village of *Tching koe* with 1,000 families.
Good blue Bricks and Tiles are made at *Tching koe*;
—the size of the former, 13 inches by 7 by 2 being
quite out of parliamentary standard. They are
half burnt as in the south. In building they are
placed edgeways—hollows of from three to nine
inches being left throughout each wall. This
mode of building is the same throughout the pro-

vince. These bricks are sold at the Kiln at 1600
Cash per thousand, or, according to their cube,
somewhat dearer than Bricks in the South.
The tiles are two cash each—also dearer then the
better burnt Kwang tung tiles.

Nor' west from *Tching koe,* distant Five *lé,* is the
village of *Chong ching* with 600 families. On the
road to it some of the cultivation is found to be taken
up with young firs. These fir sprigs are at first
planted in rows four or five inches apart, as many
as four thousand being seen in an area of twenty
yards by ten. Arrived at the age of three years
they are taken up and planted on the hills, sometimes
in little crevices over rock where nothing else
would thrive. In such a way, the hills may be
covered for miles, and where they are not so, the
ground is under preparation for them. The cultivators and proprietors of these Fir plantations have
various ways of disposing of their Crops. The first
gain is from the loppings of a certain quantity
of the branches,—then, when mature, the whole of
the branches are sold; afterwards they make sale of
the poles, with or without the bark, and lastly the
roots. Men grubbing for roots and preparing the
soil for a crop of Maize may be seen on hills of
most desperate angle. The maize stumps are not
removed, but are left to enrich the soil before firs
are again planted, or they are burnt and worms
destroyed.

To reach *Haoulung* the traveller has to retrace
the path from *Chong ching* to *Tching koe.* At
the latter place is a free ferry, a boat and hauling
line being provided by the country people for
whoever may want them. The stream here though
the water is shallow, is of considerable width, and
the traveller cannot help noticing how very much
ground is lost to the public by the inability to

restrain the streams within narrower channels.
Rather to want of pecuniary means than to lack of
engineering skill, this inability, has to be attributed.
From *Tching ko* to *Haou loong* the distance is 6¼
miles, almost due South.

Haou loong within the memory of the oldest
inhabitant in 1857 had never be n visited by foreigners, and that old gentleman, the oldest inhabitant,
one of several of eighty years of age and upwards,
was a patriarch of the Clan *Tzing*;—a clan showing
in its ancestral Hall the tablets of twenty generations. The tablets spoken of,—though alike in shape
to the tablets usually seen, *viz* pieces of half-inch
durable board, about a foot long and two or three
inches wide, with a small stand,—are here painted
green and picked with gold; the characters denot-
ing the name of the honoured spirit being also gilt.
Of one thousand families in *Haou loong* seven hundred glory in the name of *Tzing.*

The tax on land here is 450 Cash per year per
mow (6) or, according to the rate of currency, about
fourteen Shillings per acre. Neighbouring villages
pay 300 cash per mow only,—the villagers having
objected, *vi et armis*, to pay more. But the *Tzings*
are loyal men. One of their clan, in 1856, received
the degree of *Sutsai.* They look upward for the
Celestial glance, and, like sycophants all the world
over, bear uncomplainingly the burdens their more
independent countrymen resist. Four hundred
and fifty cash a mow, however, is not so high
a rate as is levied in other parts of the province.
On a professed annual value of 6,000 cash, ten per
cent is known to be taken.(7) That the land tax generally is deemed a trying burden is evidenced by
the fact that in many cases, as told of by Dr Medhurst in the account of his visit to *Teen muh sam*
in 1854, and by other writers, the landholders re-

quire bambooing before it can be got from them;
and the unfortunate proprietors hail the advent of
a revolution as a means to relieve them from payment of the impost. And with justice, indeed, may
the people complain, when, for whatever tax they
pay, they see nothing in the shape of return. The
Government, to all intents and purposes, is conducted by the people themselves. The laws of society
outraged, the offender is taken to the ancestral hall
of his clan, or to the nearest monastery. There, the
superior of his tribe, if the offender is a native, or
the superior elder if a stranger, investigates the
complaint, enforces the punishment, and at once ends
the matter. The bamboo for infliction of punishment hangs in the Monastery kitchen ready for the
culprit. There is no imprisonment—no law's delay.
When offences are really serious, as defined by
the *Ta tsing leu lee* (Code of the present dynasty) a messenger is sent to the *Yuen* or district
town with a report, and, if the offenders are several
in number, soldiers are despatched to bring them
to the *Yamun*, where the complaint being detailed
(*the investigation ends with the patriarchs*) punishment is inflicted according to the scale. (8)

Whether the incoming Government can amend
this system is doubtful, whether they will attempt
to alter it, and whether Government generally
can or will be conducted at a cheaper rate than the
present, are problems, the solution of which remains
in the womb of the future. One thing is certain—
the mode of obtaining office must be altered.
Western writers point to China's system of giving
office to men who have distinguished themselves in
a literary way as something excellent. The idea,
speaking generally, is a fallacy. No matter how
excellent a man's ability—the first office can only
be obtained by purchase after the literary degree

has been conferred;—succeeding steps by the same
means;—so that, in reality, he who can extort with
the greatest ability is the man most likely to
make his way. The present Governor of Hangchow, a detestor of foreigners, is a remarkable instance of this. Brought up in full view of the machinery of Government at *Foo chow fu* where his
father held an office only a step removed from that
of a runner, and barely enabled to compete at the
literary examinations by reason of want of qualification, (no child of a runner of a Government office
being permitted to present himself for three generations,) he has been able to raise himself,—and no
doubt but he is a man of great energy — to his
present high position. But these are the men
who form the great bars to China's progress. Once
in office they extort right and left—the man with
the longest purse, so able to buy office and play
counter foil, being the only party likely to be satisfied with the system—a system which, throughout,
flourishes on its own rottenness.

In *Haou loong* there is not one opium smoker.
Infanticide (Female) is practised occasionally by the
poorer people, but the practice is deprecated. Not
far distant from the village is a Monastery, to which
tradition assigns the residence of a dragon, but
the animal has not been seen *lately.* Seven *lê* from
Haou loong in a Sou' sou' Westerly direction is
the village of *Wan chê*, of 100 families, and four
lê further on, the village of *Neu ang koe.* The
scenery in this neighbourhood is very pleasing,—the
hills being covered with lofty firs, here and there
varied with groups of waving bamboos, which, at a
distance, appear like wreaths of cloud on a dark
back ground.

Tow vow yuen is a small place one mile from
Neu ang koe, and five *lê* further, still in a sou'

westerly direction, is the *Wong-koong ling* (Prince Duke Pass) at the top of which is a small Temple and *Ding* or rest house for travellers. The walls of this Temple are of the most simple construction, viz uprights and frame work of wood, with split bamboos interwoven daubed with mud.

Tchang koe is a good sized village in a valley S. W. from *Wong koong ling*, and from which it is distant one mile. The bed of a wide ford is passed *en-route*, over a bridge of six apertures, formed by granite uprights, the road way of the bridge being a mere split bamboo platform lashed on spars.

The *Poo-coo Ling* (Pigeon Pass) directly South from *Tchang koe*, is a tiresome ascent of over fifteen hundred feet—the mountain, a huge granite boulder, being still three or four hundred feet above the Pass. This pass marks the boundary of the *Ningpo* and *Fungwha* Districts. The view from the top is fine. Running east and west, at at a distance of eight or ten miles, is another chain of mountains, between the base of which and the *Poo-coo* mount a stream meanders under a smaller line of hills, the plain within being covered with Mulberry and tallow trees over what would be taken for pasture land, but that the few cattle foddered render such plots unnecessary. Wheat, Beans Grassicher, Clover, Peas and some Tea Bushes are all to be found here in the spring of the year—the Hills, as before told of, being studded with firs as thickly as they can stand.

Four or five *lé* from the foot of *Poo-coo* mount, in a southerly direction, is the village of *Song new haen* with a population of 300 families. A little outside the village at its entrance is a huge hollow tree, 24 feet round, the branches of which cover a space of a hundred feet and upwards.

On the way from *Song new haen* to *Shang loen-*

hing, a small temple four *lé* further south, the traveller espies, in a south easterly direction, a peculiar rock called *Ye-ling Tung san*, standing upright
between two rocks, as high, apparently, as one
of the loftiest Pagodas. This curiosity of nature
is at no great distance from the district City of *Fung
wha*. Still travelling south, *Shang yuen*, amid
a clump of bamboos, is distant one mile,—thence to
Che kaou the route inclines a little to the west
of south for some tw•o miles further.

At *Che kaou* they manufacture bricks grooved
—a device for saving material. Close by the Pot-
tery is the stream seen from *Poo coo* mount. Turning from west, a hundred feet wide, this rapid stream
is confined by a high mound from spreading over the
valley. The Pigeons giving a name to the Mountain are here seen in goodly numbers. They are of
a brown colour, their wings tipped with white. Oil
cake from Cotton seed is manufactured here in some
quantity. At the entrance of the village on a small
mound, is a pavilion to the God of Literature,
Che kaou is a thriving place of over a thousand
families, and dealers here give as many Cash in
exchange for a dollar as can be got at Ningpo; but
they do not change them willingly.

One mile west sou' west of of *Che keaou* is *Song
sah*, a small place. A Bridge over the stream
bed on the road to it is of simpler construction
than that last described—the uprights being mere
poles, with a floor of split bamboo, roughly wove.

Sing coong dong, two miles S. S. W. of *Song
sah*, lies in the route by which cattle are sent to
market from Tachow; and *Zee copoo dow*, a village
of 400 families, is four *lé* Sou' west of it.

From *Zee copoo dow* to *Tong fong she*, a village of 3000 families, the distance, still sou' westerly, is five *lé*. A tablet under a roofed bridge at this

place records the spirit of a scholar in the Sung
Dynasty of the name of *Leo dow*, who started,
with a contribution of 300,000 Cash, a project
for cutting a Canal from the adjacent River
Tong. This canal, five thousand Chang (about
thirteen miles), in length, was repaired in *Kanghe's*
reign, and an additional record planted.

The River *Tong* or *Koong Tong* spoken of is a
wide though shallow stream running from the westward. From *Ing fong sze*, a village of 300 families
by its right bank, to *Kong ling*, another village of
similar size, the distance in a westerly direction is
five *lĕ*. The water here about has a strong iron
smell. The people of the locality exhibit more than
usual energy in the construction of causeways and
embankments against the ravages of the stream.
Though unswollen by floods, this stream runs at a
rapid rate, rendering its navigation by the means employed *viz*, bamboo rafts, a work of much difficulty.
On the bamboo rafts spoken of, articles of commerce
are transported immense distances. Working against
the current they are moved singly. Laden and passing down, as many as twenty may be seen lashed
together in pairs when the stream is wide enough.
These rafts are formed of the stoutest bamboos
procurable, bent at the small ends by means of fire,
so as to form a prow three feet above the floor which
consists of some half a dozen bamboos swifted
together. By placing bundles of bamboo branches
on the top, a fine platform is constructed, and
goods of the most delicate nature, as well as pas-
sengers can be transported with speed and safety.
The agility exhibited by the prow-men with their
bamboos, in keeping the rafts in a proper direction,
is remarkable. Another description of raft is formed of short pieces of firewood, bundled in rows, like
chains,—buckling up and floating over obstacles

in its path, and righting to a level when in deeper
water.

From *Kongling,* to the three hundred family village of *Sang look,* the distance is five miles and a
third, and 2 *lĕ* further on, in the same course of S. by
W. *Sang chong* is reached, a straggling place reported as numbering a thousand families.

From *Sang chong* to *Hoĕ,* a village of 300 families, the distance Sou' sou' westerly is one mile, and
thence to *Ching kong,* a village of similar size, Sou'
west 4 *lĕ.* Tea is grown in gardens bordering the
road side here, and in some instances on the walls.
A lofty mountain bearing S. by E. called *Kou foong
san* attracts the traveller's attention at this place
and for miles onward. *Ho pĕ chee,* the next stage,
a distance of 7 *lĕ* S. S. W. is not far from its base.

In the village of *Ho pĕ chee* there are about 200
families of *Wongs* and 80 of *Sungs.* Though so short
a distance from that emporium of news Ningpo,
(under 25 miles) but little is known by the inhabitants of what is going on in the outer world. The
fact of that place having been in the hands of the
English in 1840 is not known to the common
herd; and but little desire to learn of things from
afar is indulged in even by the most educated. For
wealthy men to tell of all they know, is to lay themselves open to the squeezing propensities of the officers of their Government, by whom the most trifling matter is made use of when the game is sure.
Permission for a foreigner to reside under the same
roof for more than one night, or even for that period,
is sufficient cause for an extensive mulct. Taverns
or Monasteries are the only sleeping quarters for
travellers.

Sheong ne chee, a village of two hundred families
is only a short distance from *Ho pĕ chee.* Thence
to *Ying kow ling,* a village of 400 families, the dis-

tance in a *Sou* westerly direction, is seven *lé*.
Travellers from the west will be pleased and interested at seeing here a specimen of bridge building
such as they will not have expected. The stones of
which it is composed are as rough as they grew,
and placed so compactly in an arch of 23 feet span
that not one stone is out of line; the skill of the build-
ers in fixing the keys evincing a knowledge of engineering principles for which Chinese are seldom cre-
dited. The road way over the top is prettily tesselat-
ed. This style of cobbled arch is not uncommon in
other parts of the province,—the smaller brooks in
many places being so bridged over.

Ying kow ling, too, is in the great market
thoroughfare;—fowl carriers and drovers being met
in such numbers, occasionally, that the road is block-
ed up with them.

Shit dee deo, about 14 *lé* south from *Ying
kong ling*, is the residence of a Shanghae dealer
speaking English, of the name of *Adjing*. Travel
lers this road will find a ready welcome at his
house. *Fah shong ling* is a hamlet of a hundred
families not far from the place last mentioned.
A Temple here is called the *Wong koo mew*.
Moehang, a village of a similar size is about two
miles from *Chin kiy ling* (Front road pass) and
here is a small Temple, where a *Hoshang*, (Buddhist
priest) supplies hot tea gratis to all who wish it; the
cost of the establishment being defrayed by the people
of the village, a place numbering 100 families. At
this point the traveller finds himself in the hill region, and enjoying lovely scenery,

Yung ko jo and *Sing ko jo* are each villages
of 100 families between the pass last mentioned
and a very steep and high pass called *Kwei ling
foong*, the boundary of the *Fung wha* and *Sing
chong* districts.

The remarkable way in which the hills are covered with Fir or other timber here, not an inch of available ground being left unimproved, has much to do in convincing the sceptical that for future generations there is little room—China is full;—*for her increasing population there must be an outlet* or other modes must be invented whereby they may gain existence. If mines could be opened in places of known mineral production, a great relief might be obtained.

The view from the top of the *Kwei-ling-foong* and from the *Jong-kong-ling* temple, a little way down the hill, is grand to a degree. In a W. S. W'ly direction the mountains are very high. Tea is grown on the hills here in some quantities, and bamboo trees in much greater.

The ascent of the *Kwei-ling-foong* occupies nearly an hour of trying travelling. At the base on the western side, is another temple, *Kwei-ah-Deen*, with a free tea table;—Prince and peasant, rich and poor, being equally welcome to a bamboo noggin of the beverage "which cheers but not inebriates."

The village of *New-Za* is five miles, in a sou' westerly direction, from the Temple on the mount; —and five miles further, W. S. W. is the *Poosan* Monastery. On the road to this place are four Bridges, constructed by public subscription in the 3rd year of Taoukwang (as told of in a tablet by a small shrine to the God of waters, opposite *Rhinoceros* mount) the *Chang* family heading the list of contributors, a member of the clan, though professing his ability to be small, writing the inscription, and setting forth the reasons for the construction of the works.—One of these bridges, *Toong-jow*, is a specimen of many others in the province, constructed of granite stones, three or four feet

long, dressed to a curve, and built up latitudinally.
Thus, from the floor to the crown of this bridge, of 18
feet span, there are only three stones on one side and
two, where the side rests on a rock, on the other;
—the whole arch being built with about thirty
dressed blocks, packed on the haunches with un-
hewn stones from the brook below.

Some remarkable sand cliffs, one called precipice
gate, are to be seen here, and the mineralogist will
find materials for research in the various soils of
purple, red and other colours in the neighbourhood.

There are five resident priests at the *Poosan*
monastery;—the Abbot's name is *King-chuen*. Mon-
astic lands (the Poosan Monastery possessing 100
mow,) are not exempt from the customary impost.

Ten miles (30 *lě*) N. W. from the *Poosan* Monastery are the hills from which iron sand washes
into the stream bed below. This sand is smelted into
pigs' at various places in the vicinity. There are
one or two such smelteries close by the *Kwei-ah-
Deen* (the Temple spoken of at the foot of the *Kwei-
ling-foong*) and the traveller may be interested in
visiting them as well as the mines. The furnaces are
simple upright clay cylinders, similar to those used
for casting purposes in the south of China. The
sand yields of pure ore-two thirds of its gross weight
(66 in 100) which, cast in pigs of 3 catties each,
sells at the furnace for 32 cash a catty, about
equal to £12 per Ton of 20 Cwt. (9) They smelt 700
péculs a year at this place, the residence of 100
families.

Leaving the village of *New-Za* for the mines,—
about a mile nor' west is the hamlet of *Chang-woo*
with 40 families, and one mile north again is *Djee
Deo* with 100 families. The women here dress
their hair in a peculiar manner. In front it is brush-

ed back as in the south, but the back hair is twisted
in a roll, and bound tightly from the poll with black
silk cord for a length of 7 or 8 inches.(10) This is then
turned up, like a horn, at the back of the head, and
stands four or five inches above the crown, the hair
then being turned round, so as to give it the appearance of a handle. In cases where, instead of being upright, the *horn* inclines to either side, the wearer has
quite a jaunty appearance. In the spring of 1857
foreigners had not been seen before in this quarter,
the curiosity exhibited by all on the occasion of the
first visit being something extraordinary. The style
of head dress spoken of is found to extend throughout the country from this to the River *Tsien-Tang*.

On a hill over the large village of *In-gee-coon*, of
500 families, is an hexagonal pavilion which can be
seen for some distance. *In-gee-coun* is one mile N.W.
from *Djee-Deo*, and one mile further N.W. is *Poey-
woe*, a small place of 50 families. There are two large
villages within a distance of 4 *le*, still N. W. from
Poey-woe, viz *Gan-Deo* with 150 and *Woo-Dong*
with 400 families. The houses are well built at
Woo-Dong, and it bears the appearance of a thriving place.

Tobacco is grown in this quarter, though not
largely. Travelling, by those who can afford it, is
in chairs, or rather trays, swung to a pole, the ends
of which rest on men's shoulders.

One mile N. N. W. from *Woo-Dong*, is *Kang-lew*,
a place which, besides a temple, has only a few
straggling houses. But N. N. W, thence, about
4 *le* off, is the broad bed of the stream, where, in
groups of 30 and 40 together, are the iron washers.
The iron sand as before mentioned is washed from
the hills. This is ascertained by the yield being
most prolific after the floods from the heavy rains

have subsided, say in the 1st and 2nd months of the
year, the produce in the 6th and 7th months, (the
dry season) being little, The region over which
the iron washings extend is from the village of
Tung-ling to *Wong-Zac,* a distance of ten miles
(30 *lé*) — the line, so far as it can be observed
from *Keen-che,* running N. E. and S. W. The
stream bed is over a couple of hundred yards in
width in some places, though, excepting at rain
seasons, the flow is inconsiderable; sufficient, however, to enable bamboo rafts to get to the charcoal
deposits among the mountains.

The process of iron washing is simple. The bed
of the stream, washed and unwashed, is marked
off in sections; and small channels, about a yard
wide are made from the main stream, of sufficient length to give a good fall into a wood trough
about 6 feet long and 8 inches deep, 3 feet wide at
the top and tapering to a foot and a half. Into
this trough, placed on a slight inclination, with the
water flowing over the head board, one man pours
in sand as it is brought by others, or he exhausts a
heap lying contiguous. Most of what is put in washes
away immediately, leaving behind it, however, the
sought for iron. One trough being filled, the water
is partially turned off, and another is proceeded to.
In the course of three or four hours, or less, a
trough is thoroughly drained of the superfluous
sand, and the iron grains remain. Removed in
to baskets, this is sold to the first comer at 19
cash a catty. The washers profess to earn, in good
times, as much as 200 cash a day—at others, a
mace only—little enough for such laborious work
and so much exposure. The water, about 5° of
Fahrenheit higher temperature than the air at a
spring noon—is rough to the palate and tasteless.

As it flows gontly, thé iron, though almost imperceptible to the touch, may be seen in light streaks on the yellow sand beneath. The stream here flows from the eastward, and the course to a small hamlet of 30 families called *Ding-wong*, is along its left bank for two or three *lĕ*. Half a mile further from this place the road to *Shang-chune* breaks away to the southward, through a defile clothed with firs and called *Shang-Kay-ling*. It was stated at page 12 that the *Kwei-ling-foong* was the boundary of the *Fung-wha* and *Sing-chong* Districts. There, too, commences the

DEPARTMENT OF SHAU-HING.

SHANG-CHUNE is a thriving little town, and here, at stalls by the Road side, the traveller finds excellent wheaten flour pancakes, so cheap that a hearty meal can be made of them for the merest trifle. The process of manufacturing these pancakes is simple. An earthenware pan is filled with a stiff batter of flour, water, salt and eggs, and in this the manipulators, old women generally, dip the fore fingers and spread, or rather smear the batter lightly over the hot pan ;—one spread one way, one the other, a second's delay and the food is cooked; coming from the pan as crisp and delicious as Hebrew passover cakes. Prepared in stacks a foot high, they are sold by the catty, or singly as required. Similar pancake stalls are found in and for several days of travel beyond the district city of *Sing-chong*, and are extensively patronised by way-farers from the hills A stream, not the iron washing, is met with at this place, its course from the hills being almost due south, and

though shallow is a hundred feet wide. Another
stream is crossed, too, on the road to *Tah-ming-zee,*
over a bridge of planks and trussels 250 feet in length.
Tah ming-zee, a place of 400 families, is one mile
S. W. from *Shang-chune.*—Mulberry and Tallow
tree, growing over a sandy soil, are met in several
places on the road.

    Hoi-yen, a hamlet of 30 families, is two mile sou'
west from *Tah-ming-zee.* The devotion exhibited
by the old women of this neighbourhood in telling
beads and muttering the Buddhist chant of *O-me-
to-fah* or *veh* is remarkable; and if such acts
could atone for sins or obtain the wished for good
fortune, success would be sure from the zeal displayed Occasionally, in road side temples, old women and men in threes and fours may be seen per-
petrating for themselves services prescribed in papers sold at some monastery of notoriety, and to reach
which they make extensive pilgrimages. Seated
at a table together, all repeating the mystic words
'till both tongue and brain must ache with the
repetition, one counts beads, another, at each
revolution of the string, moves from a bundle, a
sanctified joss stick, the act being signalized by
a third with a tap on a small bell, by another
with a rap on a skull-like drum, and so on until the
prescribed number of joss sticks is expended and
the service finished. Of all the intellect-stul
tifying devices superstitiously conceived, Buddhism must be the most successful. Happy the
day when the devotion now so uselessly expended is given in the exercise of a rational religion!
Speaking of them as a body, the Chinese are, in-
trinsically, a very God fearing people, and Christianity once introduced will have ardent and faithful
practisers.

From *Hoi-yen* to *Fong-quong-ling*, a *Ding* on a hill, which, with its arched verandah and white washed walls is seen from a good distance, the course is S. W. one mile. From the top of the *Ling*, *Sze-ming-shan*, a mountain 2,500 feet high, bears N. by W,distant some fifteen miles.. From the top of *Sze-ming-shan* a view is obtained of three departments at a glance, *viz* Ningpo, Taechow and Shaouhing. *San-Tew*, a small hamlet of 30 families on the top of this hill, surrounded by tea bushes, is W. S. W. 5 *lĕ* from the ding spoken of. From this spot, as far as the cye can reach all round, only mountains meet the view. A little way down the hill, southerly, is the village of *Wong-mo-teah*, of 100 families, 10 *lĕ* from which, due west of the village, is the district city of *Sing-chong*.

The great object of attraction at Sing chong is the *Tow-va-sze*, or Temple of the *Great Buddha*; and to reach it, travellers from the east pass through the city and mount a sharp ascent in the rear; then descending a flight of steps to the other side, a total distance from the city walls of 4 *lĕ*. A monastery of 50 priests is attached to the Temple, and, by the Abbot and Guest chancellor, the latter particularly, every attention and kindness are readily given to foreign visitors. A more fortunate selection for such an establishment could not have been made. It is in a complete hollow amid a group of hills and precipitous rocks from one to two hundred feet high, just large enough for the Monastery and outbuildings, the approaches winding in such a way that, but for a knowledge of the existence of the place, it would not easily be discovered. Here, carved out of the solid rock, fifty one feet in height from the base on which the demi-body sits, the great Buddh is arched in and enthroned in truly god-like state.

The rock out of which the idol is cut, (a conglomerate—porphyritic—resembling a hard gray green free stone) is about a hundred feet high with a N. E'ly aspect.

From the front of the knees (the figure being sculptured as sitting cross legged) the depth back is 29 feet, the recess being smoothly coved up until it meets in a lozenge arch three feet above the crown of the idol's head. Springing from walls rising 29 feet above the floor, and meeting, on its inner face, the natural rock, is an artificial well turned arch of curved stones, 46 feet in span, extending out and forming 25 feet of the roof of the temple, which, on the floor, is 46 feet square. The table on which the idol sits is 5½ feet from the floor, the whole height of the temple being 58 feet to the crown of the recess. Stout granite columns support the verandah forming the exterior of the Hall. Along the walls, on each side, are alcoves, with ten idols in each, of somewhat less than human size. In the centre of the area, 7½ feet from the great Buddha, on a table 8 feet square, is a very jolly representation of the god *Me-doe*, 6 feet 6 inches high from his seat, supported on either side by the unfinished halves of two figures, intended, when complete, to be 18 feet high.

Excepting that the ears are extraordinarily long, the great Buddh is modelled in regular proportion. In the palm of the right hand, the fore finger of which measures 6 feet 6 inches in length, is an image on a pedestal. This image, viewed from the end of the temple, appears as diminutive as a doll. On measurement, however, it proves to be, with the pedestal, 2 feet 8 inches high. The great Buddha in order to make it smooth enough for gilding, is, in places, thickly plastered. The head is carved to the appearance of a skull cap, studded with fir nuts, with a round space over the forehead, painted partly red, partly brown, similar colours with blue decorating the head dress. Between the eye brows stands a large round jade, and in the centre of the bare breast, the brasitica or character 卍 is depicted, studded with blue drops. The gilding, though bright, is thin and well executed; the folds of the garments and bands being picked with vermillion, as also are the lips of the image. The countenance is pleasing. The width over the knees on the seat is 36 feet. In a halo over the head, the recess is coloured to a purple brown, the rest of the coving and the artificial arch being white-washed.

Of the history of this idol the monks know little (11); but tradition assigns its sculpture to the time of the *Leang* Dynasty (A. D. 550) The tomb of the first high priest is shown close by the temple, under some trees, and is pointed to with much veneration. A cave in a rock above the temple is also said to contain the books and remains of a studious old priest. The monks speak of a fire so intense as to have destroyed the fingers of the image as at first carved, and of the plunder of a precious gem, erst in the place of the present jade between the eyebrows;—circumstances leading to the conclusion that in days gone by there were ruthless men as little disposed to pay respect to Buddha as the present iconoclastic followers of Tai-ping-WANG.

Attached to the Monastery are 150 mow of land, for which the priests pay government annually 250 cash a mow.—Altogether they pay the state 60 Taels per annum. On the exterior of the great temple are the following inscriptions. Over the lower verandah 殿寶雄大 *Tah-yeong-pow-tea,*

Over the second story 蹟聖生三 *Sam-sing-seng-cheh.* Between the second and third 樓遙道 *Seaou-yun-laou,* and over the fourth 天洞勒彌 *Me-leh-tong-tien,* whilst within, on either side of the Image are the following—佛尊勒彌 *Chuey-sing-chong-mie,*—嚴莊勝最 *Me-le-ching-veh,* (12).

On the right of the entrance to the Monastery are two caves. One of these, an aperture some 22 feet high, 30 deep and 35 wide, is dedicated to the goddess of mercy, with whose image, attended by some two dozen others, one of them a monkey, the cave is adorned. The other cave, some 40 feet wide at the entrance, is appropriated to a representation of *Che-foo-tsze,* and to some comfortable apartments for priests. The name of *Che-foo-tsze,* the founder, some seven or eight hundred years ago, of the Chinese atheistic school, from characters said to have been written by himself, is engraved on a rock outside the cave a short distance from the Monastery, On the right of the flight of steps from the hill top is another cave about 80 feet wide, 30 deep, and 16 high. No less than one thousand images line the walls of this place, mere dolls for the most part, recessed in mud daubings around a gentleman of large proportions in the centre. The priest in attendance here is an intelligent and thrifty old man, speaking with an evident sense of self merit at having been able to build a house and purchase some 25 mow of ground out of the contributions of devotees at the shrine of which he is in charge.

The antiquarian finds much to interest him in the neighbourhood of the Monastery; and does not overlook the ruins of a pavilion and tomb close by, —a horse and dragon on the latter, though still in good relief, indicating the hand of a sculptor of many centuries past.

The walls of the City of *Sing-chong,* upwards of three miles in circumference, and of the average height of Chinese city walls, are solidly built of dressed granite, with brick battlements, and are in good preservation, flanging in somewhat like the sides of an old fashioned ship. The shape of the city is that of a long lozenge, smallest on its northern end. As customary, there are gates at each of the cardinal points. Much of the space within the walls, especially away from the centre, is occupied with mulberry trees, and vegetable gardens within neichune walled compounds, one and two hundred feet square. The battlements, lining a road-way from 12 to 15 feet wide, are pierced for gingalls only;—but none of these implements, nor any other kind of artillery, are mounted in peaceful times. The foreigner, as an object of curiosity, creates about him, as a matter of course, huge crowds of obstreperous boys and wonder seekers, —but they are not vicious, and give vent to no such obscene and insulting expressions as are continually heard in the south.

The street leading through the city from the gate at the nor' west corner, is well lined with market stalls, though not much has to be remarked of the wealth or business of the inhabitants. For instance, there is no silver-smith shop; the first established luxury *dépôt* even in a fishing village in Kwangtung. Still the people look fat and contented; and but few beggars are seen. At established money changers, Carolus dollars, 10 per cent better then Mexican, yield from 1020 to 1030 cash each— a trifle only under the rate obtainable at Ningpo. A respectable looking ten cash piece is current here and in the immediate neighbourhood; but it is useless for the traveller to burden himself

with many of them; for a few miles further on they
are received unwillingly, or are altogether rejected.
These coins, though bearing the present Emperor's
name both in Chinese and Manchou characters, are
said to be the production of private mints;—the professed objection to their receipt being that they
are cast of an inferior metal and below the Imperial touch.   Only the Carolus dollar will be received in change at any of the cities,—Mexican or
other stamps being repudiated.

The temples, the only fine buildings at Sing
chong, are without the walls.   The river bed
which, at a distance from it of from one to two
hundred feet, runs along the eastern wall, though
shallow generally, is wide.   In fact it is a double
stream crossed from the east for lengths of two
to three hundred feet each, with two bridges
of stout planks and trussels.   Between the stream
and the wall the ground is covered with Mulberry and Tallow trees, over wheat and other
cultivation.   Indigo is cultivated in this region
too.   A short distance west of the city is a seminary for the education of respectable youth,—and a
little beyond it may be seen a five storied pagoda,
crowning a hill overlooking the road from *Sing-
chong* to *Dzing*.   This pagoda marks the boundary of the Sing chong district.

Dzing, or Dzing *Yuen, Yuen* or *heen* signifying
the chief city of a district,—lies about N. W. from
Sing chong yuen ;—though for a third or so of the
distance of twelve miles between the two places, the
road runs to the southward of west into a plain.
Ten *lè* from the *Tow-va-sze,* is the hamlet of *San-
chee* of Thirty families ;—Four *lè* further, W. by
N. is *So-chee-deo,* a hamlet of similar size ; and
Dow-chee, a village of 100 families lies a little be-

yond. The European traveller has no reason to complain of difficulty in getting along in this quarter. *Dings,* substantially roofed sheds, through which the roads run, open to all, are to be found at nearly every mile, and within them, or not far distant, are shops for the sale of good wheaten flour pancakes at two cash each, fresh boiled sweet potatoes at five cash a catty, rice congee at 2 cash the half pint basin, and a liquor not unlike stale small beer, a potation not over agreeable to all palates, fermented from rice, and sold hot at eight cash the gill. Hot gruel stands ready in some of the *dings,* Chinese taking it either as gruel at 2 cash the half pint basin, or, flavoured with soy, chopped onions and small dried shrimps as a soup, at 3 cash the basin. Half a dozen of the pancakes, and a couple of basins of the soup, form a good meal for a moderate man, and with five cash worth of tea can be obtained at a total of something under twelve cash a penny. Hot water standing ready, the five cash worth of tea has a good many brewings when the traveller is thirsty before the leaves are thrown away.

The plain between Singchong and Dzing, bounded by huge granite bouldered hills, is studded with numerous villages—the stream bed winding here and there among the mulberry trees deep enough for bamboo rafts laden with bean cake and charcoal for more eastern markets

Two *lê* W. by N. from *Dow-chee* is *Wong-nee-joh* a small hamlet of 20 families, and a *lê* N.W. is *Yuen maou,* with 50 families. Many of the inhabitants of this quarter appear to be blind, or weak in the eyes; and no greater kindness can be shown to the poor creatures in passing than the gift of small parcels of blue vitriol, with written directions for dilution and use.

Dzing-yuen, is seventeen *lĕ*, nearly six miles, due north from *Yuen-maou*, over a splendid road, wide enough for a carriage and pair with outriders; —the surrounding country being not unlike the small arable downs of England. Approaching *Dzing*, the stream is again met running shallow and fast from the westward; crossing which the road, through groves and hedge rows of bamboos and mulberry trees, and fields of wheat and barley, is a perfect zig-zag, until it reaches a wider and deeper stream, crossed by a substantial starlinged bridge.

On the southern bank of the stream, skirting the suburbs of *Dzing*, is a small monastery, in which the foreign traveller can obtain quarters, though less luxurious than those of the *Tow-va-sze*. A tablet here records the setting off of a large tract of the river for the preservation of life; and fishing within it, in order that life may be sustained, is not allowed.

Very good boiled bread, in not less than four catties at a boiling, can be obtained at Dzing, if ordered over night, at 40 cash per catty. Buffalo milk is procurable too occasionally. The city walls, some three or four miles in extent, are in good condition ; on the northern face running sharply up a hill for a considerable distance. Dzing is a quiet place, with the character of being the abode of many of the literati. Of general business there appears to be but little. A temple to Confucius, and some excellently carved stone work, are objects of attraction in the centre of the town. The condemnable custom of leaving the coffins of the dead above ground, is not practised here so freely as at Ningpo and other parts of the province; and for miles the hills in the spring time are seen

covered with the white and pink flowers of plum
and peach trees, among waving bamboos and small
firs, over wheat, beans and clover.

With its character for learning, Dzing, too,
as a consequence, perhaps, (after the classic wit-
ticism " Port wine and Greek ") is said to har-
bour many opium smokers. Outside the abodes of
such, however, but little of the effect of the practice
is seen; and though all may be true that is told by
missionary travellers of the result of their observations, it is a singular fact that plain men of the
world in China have to strain both their optic and
their olfactory nerves to discover that opium is at
all made use of. This fact, however, is no answer
to the many excellent and sage observations of those
who entertain a *penchant* for condemning the use
of luxuries to which they, themselves, have no inclination.

Dzing, like most of the other district cities has
much cultivated ground within its walls, and, excepting that such places afford a shelter to officers of Government, and aid in perpetuating the tyranny of
the rulers, the benefit accorded to the people by the
existence of walled cities is problematical. There
was a time, perhaps, when the richest men of the provinces were quartered within them; and there are indications of such a time in many of the houses now
used for the commonest purposes. Taverns (*Van-
teens*) in the suburbs,—failing monasteries, the only
quarters for the foreign traveller—are often found
to be well arranged houses, with open courts in the
centres, and avenues and partitioned rooms—built,
evidently, for people who had some sense of taste
and decency; but now, Oh, how filthy and begrim-
ed with dust! That a quiet, easily contented people are borne by their government to the ground

with a more than night mare-weight, and crushed
of all spirit for a higher order of enjoyment than
that possessed by the brute creature, is proclaimed at every step in silent speaking language, more
eloquent than the wail of the western slave.

From *Dzing-yuen* to *Coong-dong*, a village of
a hundred families on the top of a hill, the distance
is seven *lĕ* west. The next place reached, N. W.
four miles, is *Sing-coon-you*, a hamlet of 50 families. From the road way, in the centre of a semi-
circle of hills, the valley below, in a southerly and
westerly direction, is studded with numerous villages and white washed houses, many of them,
apparently, the dwellings of the workers among
the huge groups of mountains adjacent. *Mosen-
shee* one mile N. W. of *Sing-coon-you*, lies a little
to the left of the road. It is a village said to
number over 400 families. Thence to *Tsung-jin*
the course is W. N. W. for about two miles.
Tsung-jin, is an extensive village or township of
over 3,000 families. Among other curiosities in this
quarter, wild cat, fox, and bear skins are obtainable; and in the spring a small fruit of a pleasantly
sour flavour, different from any seen in other parts of
China. Joss stick and bricks are made here, and
much of the native manufactured cloth is dyed.
The bed of a shallow stream running from the
north at this place, is over 250 feet in width, and is
crossed by a bridge of nine starlinged piers. But
though so flourishing a place, the dealers object
to giving cash in exchange for foreign dollars;—
they say, as is said at nearly all the inland villages,
they do not want silver, and would rather lose the
sale of their goods than make what they deem such
a barter exchange. Some fine elm like trees, called *Fung-jee*, are to be seen in this quarter;—the as-

pect of the region being that of a picturesque woodland; interspersed with what foreigners are used to
call triumphal arches. These are square stone uprights, with lintels and plinths, intended to comme-
morate the virtue of some by-gone hero, or heroine.
Widows who have lived virtuously are much honoured after their decease by memorials of this kind;
indeed the majority of these ornaments appear to
have been erected for such a purpose.

Still continuing W. N. W. the road runs over
one or two hills on which tea is grown, though
not in large quantities, for five miles until the
foot of the pass called *Shih-meaou-ling* is reached. Here, for at least one good day's plodding,
the traveller bids adieu to level country, and
mounts and descends flights of steps and rugged
paths till head and foot are well a-weary. Straw
shoes for Chinese pedestrians are in great demand
here. The price of them, with straw wisp sandals,
is only ten cash, or under a half-penny a pair. For
baggage carriers they are a bad substitute for a
shield to the foot, and are apt to cut the toes or
create blisters. The women in this quarter, even
of the poorest class, wear head ornaments of
jade stone set in gold and blue feathers, resembling lockets, in the centre of a tiara of black silk,
satin, or common cloth; and though used to working
in the fields with the men, are all cramped into the
detestable small foot system.

Half a dozen miles beyond the pass is the village of *Keu-zhin* of 100 families. At this place
there is a temple, and two fine arched bridges of
cobbled stone. After leaving *Keu-zhin* the road
runs through a rocky glen, with one or two beautiful water falls, to the hamlet of *Seang-ming*, of
30 families. The distance from *Keu-zhin* to this

place is about a mile and a third N. W.—West again, distant four miles, is the *San-moong-ling* to reach which, the road, very narrow, skirts the sides of mountains of frightful acclivity, studded from bottom to top with some of the loftiest bamboo trees in the world, here and there, on western sides, over patches of tea trees. It is hardly safe to attempt riding in a chair in this quarter; but in no part of the world can the beauty of the scenery through which the traveller passes, until he reaches the hamlet of *Shih-chong*, be exceeded; the streams in the glens below being of considerable width, winding principally from the N. W. and running, angrily, to the southward, as though they hastened to become the fathers of useful rivers.

Shih-chong numbers some 60 families, all of them engaged in the manufacture of a coarse quality bamboo paper. The bamboos used for this purpose are usually two years old. Split and cut into three foot lengths, they are placed in vats, in some cases covered with lime, and left to soak in water until almost rotten. Some of these bamboo cuttings remain in vat for eight and nine months before using. This, however, is a long period, and one and two months are enough to render the pith of the bamboo fit for the water-power-worked pounding hammer. The process of manufacturing the paper is similar to that in the west. The pulp is thrown into vats which are fed with water through shoots leading from the hill streams, the pulp being taken up on fine bamboo screens. One pair of hands is able to throw off as many as 300 sheets an hour; a pile of 8 feet high, of sheets 2½ by 1 foot square, being a fair day's work. The machine for expressing the water from the pile is clumsy enough, but effectual in reducing

it to about a fourth of its cube. The drying houses
are low buildings with walled ovens in the centres,
and fed from the outside. To the exterior of these
walls, as they slightly slope in from the base, the
sheets are lightly pressed, and left until they dry
and drop off, after which they are placed in stack,
ready for market. This paper is often used in
the lieu of horse-hair or straw for plaster work, and
sells for 2,400 cash per pecul of 100 catties. A good
deal of paper is made from straw, too, in this quarter,
and also farther along on the borders of the River
Tsien-tang. The good white paper seen in Shanghae is manufactured at Soo-chow, and, though of
better fabric, is dearer than that made in the south.

From *Shih-chong*, still travelling W. N. W. the
road runs through a continuous series of mountain
passes; the rocks in some places lying up and down
in heaps in admired confusion;—foaming brooks
and water-falls adding the highest grace to the al!-
romantic scenery. Some of the timber cut here re-
sembles the beech for closeness of grain, and would
serve admirably for stocks for carriage wheels. In
lengths of ten and twelve-feet, large stacks of it are
to be seen in the streams, or on their banks awaiting
transport to a mart. So difficult is it for the charcoal carriers and native travellers in these defiles
to obtain food, that they usually carry it, (cold rice
and greens,) in small bags, and eat by the way side.

Nieu-koh-san four miles and a third from *Shih-
chong*, is a small hamlet of 20 families; and, still
ascending—still ascending—the next place reached,
Tan-chay-woo, by a small arched bridge, numbers
only three families. At the *Ding* here, the traveller misses the customary idol; but in place of it
finds paintings of gods and goddesses,—red capped
and clubbed hunters, and venerable ladies. The

Ethnologist travelling through Chekiang finds
much subject for working on in the marked ten-
dency of the people to varied forms of worship.
In each district there is more or less of supersti-
tion of a kind different from that of its neighbour.
At one section the *dings* have small, at others, large
idols;—at one, one class of paintings, at another,
another class;—and northward, between the provinces of Anwhuy and Kiangsu, both idols and paintings disappear. It is hard for a foreigner to predi-
cate from the disposition of the people in one province
what is likely to be expected in the province adjoining. In one district the inhabitants are highly phi-
lanthropic, keeping tea ready for the traveller's com
fort, with payment to a priest to see that the kettle
boils;—in another the tea has to be paid for; but in
all the districts we are writing of, there is a lauda-
ble spirit of treating each other kindly, and doing
for the neighbour what they would have done for
themselves.

The broad mountain stream from the west is
met at *Tan-chay-woo* by another stream from the
north, following whose left bank the traveller, at
two *lé* distance, arrives at *Sun-chay-woo*, the location of 2 or 3 families engaged in smelting iron
sand; and a little further on is *Djing-kong*, a hamlet
of 30 families, near the foot of a pass called *Shang
coo-ling*. A farinaceous article called *Leong-cha-
kee*, is procured from the thin black roots of a fern
growing in this quarter. Woman and children are
the manipulators, by beating the roots, which have
an oily smell, on stones by the way side. Tea is
grown in some quantity on the tops of the hills here;
the ascents rising at an average of four feet in ten.

Descending, the course is about N. N. W. for one
mile to the village of *Shee-kong*, of 150 families,

and thence, still descending, trending somewhat to the southward of west for about seven *lê*, a *Ding* is arrived at, marking the boundary between the districts of Dzino and Tchi-ki.

So utilitarian are the Chinese in all their productions, that, on viewing the marked difference in the aspect of the foliage on the approach to the Tchi-ki district, the traveller is induced to stop by the descending way to enquire into the character of the massive trees, with ferny branches of a deep olive green not unlike those of the old Yew of England. Trees of this description are cultivated in large numbers and cut into excellent planking.

The Landscape painter, for a picture here, has to exhaust his pallet. The soil, of a red brown, is in parts cut up for planting ; in others covered with the yellow flowered *brassica* before spoken of, or with maize or sedges;—then the limner has the green of wheat, the deeper tinted tea, the gold and silver wreathed bamboo, and the dark olive of the yew tree ;—the hills, in some parts, rising perpendicularly from the stream bed below, and continually inducing in the lover of nature in its rugged forms, an exclamation of pleasure and surprise.

Fong-jue-ling, is the name of the pass between the boundary of the districts and a little location called *Tchin-za-dow,* 5 miles N.W. from the village of *Shoe-kong,* where one or two families are employed in the manufactory of paper. From *Tchin-za-dow* to *Ching-ka-wo,* a hamlet of 40 families, the course is N.N.E. one mile. A fine open ancestral hill is to be seen here ; and from the appearance of the exteriors of the little two storied whitewashed houses, with indented window lintels and ornamented gables, the inhabitants might reasonably be expected to possess more desire for cleanliness within their dwellings. Dirt and filth, however, are all their ornament;—the comfort of furniture, indeed, is sparingly indulged in by Chinese.

From this place to *Che-kew*, a village of a hundred families, the course is north, distant one mile. Good, sweet, crisp, finger shaped biscuits can be bought here at two cash each. By a three piered Bridge on the road side there are several bamboo crushing mills for paper making. *Sah-keo*, a village of 150 families, N. by W. five *lĕ* from *Che-kew*, is the first patch of houses on the plain. By a small temple outside there is a fine Camphor tree, of large size; the surrounding country being covered with mulberry and other trees of loftier growth.

From *Sah-keo* to *Shae-fah*, and beyond it, the paved cause-way is wide enough for a carriage, and is kept in excellent repair. *Shae-fah* numbers 550 families, and *Woo-jaw*, a little further on, 700 families. The houses, of a superior class, are walled in here, and from the number of celebration columns seen, and other indications, the inhabitants appear to be above the ordinary standing. *Loo-'ngh* is a hamlet of 20 families two miles N. W. from *Woo-jaw*; and 5 *lĕ* further, W. N. W. is *Zoo-tow* of 50 families.

At *Loo'ngh* is a fine two storied temple;—the country around exhibiting some lofty firs and low poplars; the hills in early spring being covered with azalias of wild growth. N.W. of *Zoo-tow*, on a hill, is a square pagoda of five stories. A sixth story has fallen off just over the uppermost window, so giving to the top of the pagoda the appearance of a battlemented tower. On measurement, this pagoda, built of brick, is found to be 13 feet square outside, the lower walls 3 feet 9 inches thick, lower

story 13 feet high, and the other stories of similar
height apparently.

Immediately beneath the pagoda, N. W. is
the town of *Fong-je-how*, and further on in a.
nor' westerly direction are a series of lakes and
winding streams between the hills and the River
Tsien-tang. On the south foot of the hill under
the pagoda is a capacious monastery, with good accomodation for the foreign traveller if he require it.
But at *Foong-je-how* there are three firms, *viz* the
Wan-ho, the *Ling-jin*, and the *Ta-heu*, all doing a
stirring business in tea and silk with the northern
consular Ports. The head of the first named, a gentlemen of the name of *Luh-ching woo*, (11) is prone to
hospitality, and will not permit the foreigner to remain at the monastery outside.

From Mr *Luh* or his brothers, the traveller
may gain much useful and interesting information. From him it was learnt that though there
were as many as 5,000 families in the town, say
25,000 people, there was not one officer of government; and as this place may be taken as an index to towns of similar size throughout the country,
we here see upon what erroneous bases we speak
when we say that to destroy the government, as
established in a walled city, we leave nothing to
follow but anarchy for the mass. * In reality, as
before stated, the people of China govern them-

* The *Weekly Despatch* of the 1st. February 1857. thus remarks on the then recents acts of war at Canton. —
"And now having destroyed the Chinese Government, and
brought chaos upon 350 millions of people, will Ministers tell us
whether they are prepared to substitute another ruling power for
that they have destroyed? Do we propose to annex China, or
to partition it among the friends of the "sick man," American,
French and English? Are we really aware what we are about
when we take from countless millions their recognised rulers

selves ; and no blows that may be directed at provincial heads, will affect, so far as the general well
being of society is concerned, the condition of the
masses ;—provided always that our blows are not so
directed and so continuous as to prostrate the whole
fabric ; and to destroy that supreme police for which
Governments, even of the worst class, are tolerated.

By the ancestral hall of this family (a capacious
building exhibiting the tablets of twenty four generations of the clan *Luh,*) the firm of *Wan-ho* have
their manufactory for the tea known to the trade
as the *Ping-suey,* a green of excellent character.
Until the fourth month of the year, when the gather-
ing commences, the 120 drying pans of the *Wan-
ho* establishment are filled with paddy husk, to prevent them from rusting, and nothing is done, beyond the manufacture of the boxes. From *Fong-je-
how,* the depot of some surrounding miles, 270,000
pounds of Tea and 3,000 Bales, or nearly as many
pounds, of Silk, are sent annually to the foreign
markets.

These goods when destined for Shanghae are transported in boats of the capacity of a hundred chests
each, by the way of Hang chow, at which place
Teas pay a tax of 1,100 cash (nearly three farth-
ings per pound) per chest. Were these goods
taken to Ningpo direct, such duty would be avoid-
ed ; and it is to be regretted that attempts are not
made to divert some portion of the tea and silk
to a place appearing to possess equal facilities

and withdraw from this seething mass of human life the organ-
ism by which it lived ? Have we another administrative dis-
pensation to offer it in the place of that which has been fashioned
by the light of the experience of many centuries ? Do we know
what it is to undertake such a responsibility, or to throw into ut-
ter confusion all the recognised machinery of State power in such
a boundless empire ?'"

with the other Consular Ports for doing business
with dealers in the interior. At present the only
article taken in return is Sycee Silver, and it may
be, some opium. The places where opium is made
use of at Fong-je-how, however, are not publicly
known; and the foreign traveller has some difficulty in finding them out. The article, it is said, is
carried to *Fong-je-how* by the way of *Shaou-hing
foo*. Until recently, say up to the autumn of 1856,
clean Carolus dollars, in company with Sycee, were
the *media* of exchange;—but latterly there has been
such extraordinary fluctuations in the value of the
dollars, (Government edicts, perhaps, have had some
what to do with it,) that Sycee Silver or Copper cash
are the only articles in which, as a rule, value is
returned.

The people employed on the Tea works are all
paid after the rate of a mace a day, in hard coin; and
it is easy therefore to understand that copper cash
will be in great demand;—but over and above the
labourers' wages there must be a large surplus, and
it is to be regretted that an introduction can not
be made of our woollen goods. It would be even ad-
visable to give away woollen comforters and socks
and mits for a time in places like *Fong-je-how*,
in order to induce a fancy to such things. In cold
weather—and by common report it is cold enough
—they would be invaluable, and highly appreciated.
Up to late in the spring it is not uncommon to see
small brass hand baskets, with live ashes, carried
about from place to place, and moved from foot to
foot as requisite;—poor substitutes for the comfort
of worsted stockings.

The land tax here is after the rate of 360 cash
per mow (6½ mows, or, to be precise, 6,$\frac{4}{10}$ mows
going to an English acre) the best land letting for

3,000 cash a mow a year. But land, generally, is let to the small farmer for a per centage of the crops. What this per centage is the farmer is found unwilling to tell; and, from the various reports, and, again, from the variety in weights and measures in the several districts, there is much difficulty in arriving at truthful statistics. For a good Carolus dollar, 1100 Copper cash can be obtained;—for a Carolus 10 per cent better than a Mexican, 1010 Cash—For a Mexican dollar 920 cash. Some of the buildings at *Foong-je-how* resemble palaces; and there is an excellent specimen of masonry in a large arched bridge over the stream.

. Five *le* N. W. from *Fong-je-how*, is the hamlet of *Tchwo-San*, of 60 families; and one mile further on the hamlet of *Owydee*. Thence to the ferry and Boat station, on a canal leading to the *Tsien-tang*, the distance, still N. W. is about 2 *le*.

. The tide, which by the way of the *Tsien-Tang* flows in from Hangchow Bay, runs up the creek or canal at which the traveller from *Fong-je-how* takes boat for *Foo-yang*. These boats, of about four tons burthen, are-propelled in a curious way by a man sitting at the stern, and playing with his feet on the weighted end of a broad bladed skull. For a watch of half a dozen hours these men keep steadily at their post without any other movement than that of the feet, or a sweep right or left with an additional skull out of the stern held under the arm. The price for hire of one of these boats from the Ferry to *Foo-yang*, is 2,600 cash, together with what is called Wine money, which is a *douceur* of a mace or so for good behaviour. The general direction of the stream, though winding in some extraordinary contortions occasionally, is W.N.W. From the Ferry to where it enters the *Tsien-Tang*,

the distance is about 40 miles;—the canal in many
places passing through series of wide though shallow lakes.

About 15 miles by the stream from the Ferry, in
a nor' westerly direction, is *San-kong-keaou*, a village of 350 families. At this place two streams
meet ; one leading from *Tchi-ki-yuen*, (the chief
city of the District) from which it is distant from
15 to 20 miles,—*Sankong-keow* being a similar distance from Hang chow one way, and from the *Tsien-
tang* an other (12).

DEPARTMENT OF HANG-CHOW.
District of the Tsien-Tang.

The *Tsien-Tang*, from the embouchure of the
Feng-je-how canal to *Foo-yang*, varies in width
from one and two hundred yards to a mile and upwards; though the depth is only sufficient for vessels of light draft ;—eight or ten feet it is said, with
a tidal rise and fall of three and four feet. The
course of the stream from the canal's mouth on to
Foo-yang, is about S.W. by W. for thirty miles and
upwards. Off the city it branches off to the southward.

The country bordering the river is flat for two
or three miles inland, and for the most part covered with mulberry trees. *Foo-yang* appears to lie
in the centre of a circle of hills. On the south face
the wall reaches down to the water's edge ;—on
the east it runs sharply up an ascent, and down
as abruptly on to the north side, where the country is flatter, and but little built on; the business part of the town lying on the south. On
the western entrance to the town is a well furnish-

ed grey sandstone three arched bridge of curved
stones, the road way on the top being lined with
market stalls.. The walls of the city of *Foo-yang*
—an oblong three or four miles round—are not
in very excellent condition; and in many places
are delapidated and covered with verdure. As a
place of business, however, neither *Dzing* nor *Sing-
chong* can compare with *Foo-yang* for bustle.

A short distance north of the city is a small
temple at which a traveller could quarter, and
one mile N. by W. is the village of *Leong-van-ha.*

Thence, two *lĕ* W. N. W. is *Sing-jow* a long village of 1,500 families, inhabited principally by
straw paper makers. A branch of the *Tsien-tang* is
here crossed by a fine one arched bridge, another
branch running to the northward for a distance of 40
or 50 *lĕ*. Some excellent peppermint lozenges are
procurable here at the cheap rate of a cash each.

From *Sing-jow* to *Kwong-Djean* the distance, in
a N.W. ly direction, is four miles; though, all around,
the plain appears covered with straggling hamlets;
the white washed houses, with their step like gables,
appearing at a distance like gothic priories. The
people of this quarter speak in high terms of the
security they enjoy from plunder or attack from free
booters. Bee hives are to be seen in this quarter;—
and honey is procurable at a cheap rate. Five *lĕ* N.
W. from *Kwong-Djean* is *Suchang* a village of 200
families, and two miles further on in the same course
is *Song-jin,* a very old fashioned little place, the
inhabitants being similarly peculiar.

Five *lĕ* N. of *Song-jin* is *Yang-ko-fah* a village
of 100 families, and 2 *lĕ* further on is *Cheensoling*
of 200 families. Thence to *Cho-keu,* a hamlet of 50
families, is a short couple of *lĕ*, and a little over a
similar distance is *Loo-moe* of 200 families. Three

miles further on, still in a northerly direction, is the *Dung-Ling*, or pass marking the boundary between the *Foo-Yang* and *Yu-hong* Districts, passing over which, the traveller descends very abruptly by some large kilns for burning lime. The black lime stone rock here is almost perpen dicular;—the strata being intersected with streaks of white and red porphyry and carbonate of lime, in lines running longitudinally to the E.N.E. Blasting does not appear to be understood, and each block for the kiln is cut out with the cold chisel.

Farther down the pass, a beautiful place among the hills, is the hospitable village of *Le-shuet-sun* of 300 families, and a short distance up the glen is the *Ka-yuen-sze* a small monastery of five priests. Umbrageously sheltered, it is a dwelling which in the greatest heats of summer possesses a delicious coolness. The Superior, by the name of *Che-yuen*, is remarkably attentive to foreigners. Pumice stone, said to have been procured from neighbouring hills, is exhibited here, from which it may be inferred that the region is volcanic.

A mile from the *Ka-yuen-sze* is the *Nae-kae-ling*, a pass, marking the boundary between the *Yu-hong* and *Ling-haen* districts, and a *lĕ* and a half beyond it, is *Nieu-che-ning* the residence of two or three families—*Ning-kwo-deo*, a *lĕ* further on in a westerly direction, is another dwelling place of three or four families. The roads in this quarter are nicely laid with rough pebbles.

Fwo-paleu, a straggling village of 250 families is one *lĕ* west from *Ning-kwo-deo* ;—and on a similar course, within distances of a *lĕ* and a half from each other, still descending from the pass, are the hamlets of *Wo-chee-deo* of 60 families—*So-che-dah* of 5 or 6 families,—*In-gee-wei* of 30 families, and

Shing-fa of 5 families. Basket making is largely practised in this quarter.

The course from *In-gee-wei* to the hamlet of *Ting-yuen* of 300 families is N. W.—the distance four miles, principally through a valley over a mile and a half wide. The lime stone strata hereabout has a pitch to the N. E. of 30.° Much taste is exhibited by families in this quarter in the neatness with which they dress their children, whose blue or black jackets are prettily lined at the collars with red cloth and embroidered with black or coloured silk.

Five *le* North of *Ting-yuen* the traveller arrives at an exceedingly fine five arched Bridge built of granite, the river bed at this place being over 200 feet across. The centre arch is 31 feet span—the other arches 29 feet span—breadth 15½ feet. The stream here, running from the south, unless swollen by rains, is very shallow, and only navigable by the bamboo rafts.

Turning sharply from North to W.N.W. at four miles distant from the Bridge, the road leads over another well built three arched bridge, the stream running from west, into *Wong-sin-kwo*, a village of 300 families, over which on a hill, is a squaie five storied Brick pagoda; and N. W. by N. distant apparently 20 or 30 miles is the celebrated Mountain *Teen-muh-san* 天 日 山 (*Heaven's-eye*).

Two *le* N. W. from *Wong-sin-kwo* is the district City of *Ling-haen*, a small place; the suburbs on the N. W. side containing about as many inhabitants as the city itself, reported as having 800 families within the walls and 600 without. *Ling-haen* is one of the 1600 walled cities of which the Empire boasts. But *walled* it can hardly be called;—the boundary, of about three miles, being a mere neichune erection, seven or eight feet high and under a couple of feet thick; with gates at each of the cardinal points. Between 30 and 40,000 Bales of Silk are sent annually from this quarter, principally to the Shanghae market. For a good Carolus dollar only 980 cash can be obtained, — Rice standing at 46 cash a catty or nearly $5 a pecul. For their exports, Sycee and Opium are returned from Shanghae.

The antiquarian finds several objects of interest at Ling-haen ; one large area containing the ruins of an ancient Temple, and some lofty stone images both of the human and brute forms. The ancestral hall of the family "Tsien" is within the compound spoken of, and a tablet erected in *Kien-loong's* reign records the merits of one of the *Tsiens,* who, when the country was in a state of anarchy, after the destruction of the *Sung* dynasty, (A D 479) was a great benefactor, and almost founded a dynasty for himself (13).

In the city temple is a fine iron bell over five feet high, cast during the Ming dynasty, and bearing a motto which, translated, runs " The state pro-" tects the people—without the state there could be no tranquillity ". Some coloured images in this temple, in the habiliments of ancient dynasties, are very expressive ; a cavalier at the entrance, life size, having flowing curls, hat and dress, as nearly as possible after pictures of the gay courtiers of our Charles the 2nd's time.

Seven *lĕ* W. from *Ling-haen* is the village of *Ching-ka-teo* of 25 families and a little further on *Djui-cha* of 100 families. *Foo-ling-jow,* a village of 300 families, is one mile N.W. from it. A Bridge to cost $40,000 was commenced over the stream here (between two or three hundred feet across,) in

the beginning of the present year, 1856, and contri
butions to it are thankfully received from foreigner
as well as native passing that way (14).

The contented faces, the garden like country, the
absence of beggars, combined with fine weather, render travelling in this part of the route *delightful.*

Five *lĕ* W. by S. from *Foo-ling-jow* is the *Toong-
Mew* a large temple, and near it, low down at the
foot of a hill, may be seen, half a mile from the road,
a five storied hexagonal pagoda, white washed,
where not decayed and broke away.

Two or three Temples, are to be found at no great
distance from a hamlet of 20 families called *Shin-
chee,* at one of which, by a picturesque arched *Ding*
of superior construction, the priests offer excellent
accomodation to travellers. Tea bushes may be seen
here and there on the hills, but not in large numbers.

One *lĕ* W. of *Shin-che* is *Peau-hing-chak* a hamlet of 30 families, and Ten *lĕ* W. by N. is *Lan-pe* of
100 families. The river bed, nearly dry excepting
in the rainy season, is very wide here, and is crossed to the right bank by a seven arched Bridge of
excellent workmanship.

One mile from *Lan-pe* is *Si-long-ket* a village
of 100 families, and hence to the *Woo-loo-ling
Sze* (Monastery in the gorge) is Two *lĕ* W.N.W.

The pass above the Monastery spoken of is built
in with an arched gateway; and as the mountain
rises on each side of it and forms part of a chain
extending for a considerable distance E. and W. the
means for keeping the country safe from roving
bands are very efficient. At the bottom of the
Ling on the western side, in the *U-tsein* district
is the village of *Chow-loong* of 100 families, and by
a wide stream runing from the E. N. E. is *Lang-
kew* of 30 families. Hence to the *Vok-hing* Mon-

astery the distance W. by N. is one mile.

The number of pilgrims passing this way to the Monasteries on the eastern and western *Teen-muh sans*, give to the occupation of the priests the character of Hotel keepers. The *Szes*, indeed, should be called Caravansaries, not Monasteries. The *Vokhing* Monastery (Carvansera)is a two storied building about a hundred feet square, in the midst of a garden of mulberry trees. On the upper floor, the front rooms, with a south-eastern aspect, are in the centre left open for travellers' baggage, whilst each wing contains three large rooms, with standing bed places covered with straw for the lower order of travellers, of whom they could accomodate a hundred or so; musquito curtained beds (Oh, the Fleas!) being for the better class;—the Abbot having a room to himself, and four resident priests another.—The back rooms, commanding a view of the Eastern *Teen-muh*, are filled with lumber, winnowing machines and such like farming implements. Below, in the centre, is an open court yard,—the front hall, with an idol or two in it, being given to the use of devotees;—the back and side rooms to the accomodation of guests, as refreshment rooms, &c, whilst on the north stands the kitchen, decorated with the bamboo flogger for the refractories upon whom judgement has been passed.—Outside, again, is the bath room, in which travellers, for the cost of the fern that lights the fire, can indulge in the luxury of a hot bath, contrived simply enough in the large iron pan in which the water is boiled;— the fire being lit from the outside.

It is customary for the European traveller to give the priests a small present, say half a dollar a night for the use of the rooms;—and as the priests are money changers, giving on the average only 980

cash for the best of Carolus dollars, some little is obtained by them in the way of legitimate business. Of
the priests here there is one who has been on the
establishment twenty nine years, and from the age
of ten served a novitiate of ten years at one of the
Monasteries on the adjacent mountains. Another,
the Guest Chancellor, has been nine years a priest,
and yet so ignorant is he that he cannot write the
name of the Monastery in which he serves. A short
distance N. W. of the *Vok-hing* Monastery is a public cemetery and receptacle for dead children. Not
many, however, appear to be deposited in it;—those
who can afford it burying the remains of their
friends under brick tombs. Some of these tombs
are large enough for two or three coffins (15).

Chi-ling-jow W. N. W. of the Monastery is distant 5 *le* from it, and boasts of 40 families ; whilst
Che-ching-way-loo, 8 *le* N.W. registers 30 families.
At *Chi-ling-jow* characters painted on the walls
point the traveller to the proper roads either to the
eastern or the western *Teen-muh*,—the rule with
Chinese being directly opposite to that followed
by the English in their finger posts. The women
in this quarter dress their hair modestly, simply
tying it up behind and confining with a small
silver ornament.

The road to the Eastern *Teen-muh* is very beautiful, through groves of lofty firs and shrubbery ;
—though cultivation here is not so luxuriant as in
other parts of the province ; nor do the loftier mountains bear that profusely studded appearance so
characteristic generally of the hill scenery of Chekiang.

Ten *le* N. by W. from *Che-ching-way-loo* is the
hamlet of *Le-chin* of 50 families ; and a little further
on a comfortable Monastery or Caravansera called

Lung-zee-way-Mew-qui-deo. An intelligent look-
·ing young priest here, a lad of the name of *Sheo-
zin*, appears disposed to give much attention to the
foreign visitor;— though, in the Spring of 1857
the writer was the only one he had ever seen. His
confreres are similarly attentive, and similarly
unsophisticated.

Lung-zee-way is only a little distance from the
commencement of the ascent of the eastern *Teen-
muh*, the first *Ding* on the hill bearing W.N.W.
from the foot of the roughly laid path. Four *Dings*
are met between the hill foot and the Monastery at
the top, and are placed as follows. From the hill foot
the first *Ding* is reached in 18 minutes walking.
From *Ding* No. 1 to *Ding* No. 2 the course is
about North, and can be reached in 30 minutes.
From No. 2 to No 3 the course is about N. and of 23
minutes walking—From No. 3 to No. 4 the course
is northerly and westerly,—25 minutes walking—
Ding No. 4 is the entrance to the Monastery
grounds, and is gratefully cool.

Neither at the first nor the second *Dings* are
there any idols; only at the second there is a tablet
bearing the insciption 韋止且 (16) *Ding* No 3 has
a small idol of *Yen-Dah*, the god of wealth, sitting
on a seal like long tailed animal, and holding forward a shoe of tinsel resembling a lump of Sycee.
Ding No. 4 is a small temple with a shrine to the
god *Wei-doe*, and attended by a priest who receives
his meals from the Monastery above. Besides
the *Dings* there are several conveniently placed
stone seats under lofty firs. Should the traveller
apprehend thirst on his way up, he must not neglect
to provide himself with liquid before starting, for
though cascades are abundant enough within his
sight on the opposite side of the gorge and above,

not a dribblet is met until after he has passed the third *Ding*.

Experienced Geologists will decide, perhaps, that the Eastern *Teen-muh* and adjacent mountains are of primary, secondary and tertiary formations The strata, at the base, in layers slightly removed from a dead level, is composed of blue black slatey shale. At the height of *Ding* No. 2 the rocks resemble a brown sand stone, quite distinct from the black strata on the opposite side of the glen of similar elevation ; that strata bearing, in places, a pitch of 15, in others 50 and even 70 degrees. Between the 3d and 4th *Dings* another species of formation is met with;—and over it tea is cultivated in patches, with maize,—firs growing to great heights and of considerable girth.   On the oppos ite mountain, bamboo is the cherished tree ; not growing wildly, but regularly planted ; each plot or grove bearing marks, painted with indian ink, to distinguish it from a neighbour's stock.   Charcoal burners do a large business in these regions, the weights carried by them being far in excess of what would be borne by labourers of western lands. Provided with an iron shod staff to serve two purposes, one to help them up ascents, the other to rest one end of their shoulder stave on without placing both packs on the ground, Chekiang land carriers go over immense distances, and up trying heights, for small remuneration.

Passing *Ding* No. 4 through a grove of Fir, Cypress and Bamboo trees of splendid growth and exuberance, and still ascending, the traveller reaches the Monastery called *Chaou-Ming-Sze*, an establishment of 50 priests, and containing some fine idols ; the three principal ones being lofty god desses on lotus leaves, concealed, until the hours for worship, by yellow silk hangings.   There is a

fine brass idol too, and, singularly, in one of the
upper rooms, a white porcelain image which the
priests call the Goddess of mercy. A cross on the
breast, however, and foreign crown, at once stamp
it as a "Mary" of Roman Catholic manufacture.

To reach the western *Teen-muh*, the road has
to be retraced almost as far down the hill as the
1st *Ding*, until a path, or rather steep flight of steps
is met leading to the right, down which the traveller proceeds until he reaches first the Monastery
called *Chou-ming-haen* of five priests, and then the
village of *Tcha-se-achin* of 150 families. Here
the formation, across a woodland valley, is of red
hard sand stone,

Near *Tcha-se-achin* will be found a tomb evidently of great antiquity, embosomed in some splendid
elm like trees and other shrubbery, enlivened with
the antics of squirrels, and the music, a deep
clear note, of a very handsome long-tailed bird, to
be found only in this region. Five *lĕ* west of *Tcha-
se-achin* we reach the base of a sharp ascent called
Chou-foo-ling. After thirteen minutes walking a
small mud hut is reached, and five minutes walking
further up the steps, is a *Ding*, from which there is
a gentle descent W. S. W. to two or three houses.
The lower strata of this hill is similar to that of
the base of the Eastern *Teen-muh*, *viz* black slaty
shale, in rounded boulders of 20 and 30 feet thick
—the faces of the hills angling up as precipitously
as 40°—the strata at an angle of about 5°.

From the western base of *Chou-foo-ling* the ascent
for some distance, W.N.W. is not too steep for a chair,
until the head of a valley is reached in which five villages lie within short distances of each other, the hills
around being perfect forest wood land. *Ke-cha c*
is a small hamlet of ten families, a *lĕ* or so only from

Yee-chow-lee a village of 150 families ;—*Yat-tow-lee* again, a fine village of 300 families, being only a quarter of a *lé* or so from *Kan-se-chee* of 100 families.

The pretty manner in which children dress their hair with natural flowers among these villages is very pleasing, and the inhabitants, generally, unused to sight or speech of foreigners, whilst curious are not obtrusive, and are exceedingly kind in their deportment. It is not an unusual thing for the foreign traveller in this quarter to be politely as ked to get out of his chair *to be looked at;*— every article of dress and foreign manufacture being scrutinized with prying eyes. To pilfer or cheat appears foreign to their composition;—and loudly indeed may the foreign missionary declaim against opium'smoking, for, on a cursory glance at the habits of the people, it appears to be the only vice to which they are addicted. Of lewdness, drunkenness, quarrelsomeness, or any thing but what is pleasing in the eyes of an impartial lover of his species, nothing is seen;—nought besides opium smoking, and a want of cleanliness, is found to reform but the inclination to idolatry;—and, whilst pitying, the truly charitable can but reflect on the purit yof the source from which such propensity proceeds,—the desire to pay homage to the Supreme Being after that fashion which progenitors have taught to be the best.

Cleanliness being next to Godliness, Christianity when introduced will be a great boon. Idolatry, then, and the absence of a taste for cleanliness in their domestic arrangements, appear to be the great —almos tthe only—sins with which Chinese away from towns, have to be taxed;—the indulgence in opium smoking being seldom entered on 'till disease, or

—who shall deny it?—the desire to drown in forget
fulness a feeling of hate for the government under
which they live—renders it necessary.

The road from *Kan-se-chee* is ten feet wide, and is
well laid with pebbles and rough stones for three or
four *lē* north to a *Ding* with a shrine to the three
goddesses *Kwan-yin* 三官大帝 (17) This *Ding* is
only a short distance from another sharp ascent; and
chairs are kept for the use of lady devotees, of whom
there are many young and old arriving from all parts
of this and adjacent provinces. Here, again, in the
valley the strata is of the red brown granite like sand
stone spoken of ;—whilst a little way up the hill it
is black shale and lime stone. At the top of the ascent
called *Le-do-ling*, there is a one priested Temple,
at which pedlar brokers meet to purchase from villagers leaves resembling the mulberry leaf in shape,
called 青霜葉 *Tching-sha-yet* (18). These leaves,
suffused in boiling water, yield a pleasant cool-
ing drink. In quantities, the dealers obtain them
at three cash a tael, or about half a mace a catty.

To preserve them from the effects of the sun,
wood cutters in this region wrap the head with blue
cotton cloth of native fabric. European manufactured cloths, blue, white or gray, are not to
be seen in this locality; and yet there must be much
room for them, if there could but be an introduction.
Not that for actual durability anything can excel
the substantial cottons made by the thrifty house
wives.—Sold, however, at a price commensurate with
the labour given to them, they are, excepting in
scant quantity, above the means of the little earning
labourer.

Who shall describe the beautiful wood land dell
through which the traveller passes from the *Le-do-*

Ling down to the great Monastery (the *Choey-yen-sze*) at the foot of the Western *Teen-muh san* ? Cypress and Fir, planted in regular lines over the green sward, or little hills of wheat, are the principal features.

The *Choey-yen-sze* is the most remarkable establishment of its kind for many a league around. It was originally founded, by the priests' account, in the Sung Dynasty (A.D. 420) (18) and will have continually increased until now it numbers on its foundation four hundred priests and a hundred laymen. Its situation, within an amphitheatre of wooded mountains, is most beautiful;—and should it at any time be necessary to fix the head quarters of an embassy, or to found a seminary in this locality, by no possibility could a better site be selected.

The principal entrance of the *Sze* faces the south, the depth from the portico to the northern wall being 575 feet, with a mean breadth in the centre of 425 feet, the corners rounding of with an easy sweep. Fronting the portico is a semi-circular paved area, 122 feet wide and 72 feet deep, bounded by a moat, or ha-ha, beyond which the ground is cultivated as a kitchen garden. Within the entrance from the front area is a spacious court yard, 70 feet wide by 100 feet in depth, with a flight of steps to the reception hall. Thence is another court yard, about the same size as the other, but with three flights of steps, leading into a temple of a secondary class ; branching from which, on the west, are dormitories for the better class of guests ; and on the east, the refectories of devotees and priests. Beyond this temple, still proceeding north, is another court yard leading to a capacious hall, beyond that again being another court with a large censer, and then the principal Temple—a Shrine to the three goddesses *Kwan-yin*

In the rear of this Temple a verandah runs across from one side to the other over a length of 220 feet. This verandah fronts several smaller two storied temples, and altar pieces ;—in the rear being another range of five temples, with smaller ones behind these again, and then a small kitchen garden, bounded by the Monastery wall and hedge. This boundary in its whole extent embraces an area of five and a half acres of ground. On the west side, besides the dormitories spoken of is a fine kitchen garden—on the east are buildings of various classes. A gate on the north east corner leads into a road way by a perfect street of two storied houses, at the end of which is the grand kitchen, a building in which the boilers for rice measure six feet across, with scoops to remove the food not unlike the ladles used in iron foundries. Adjacent to the *cuisine* is a large two storied Hall, with an open area a hundred feet square, and a rostrum, intended, apparently, for the purpose of addressing a multitude. Such a building, now almost altogether unoccupied, would afford several companies of soldiers the most comfortable quarters. The south eastern quarter of the compound—the eastern side of the entrance courts mentioned being twice as wide as the western areas—is variously bestowed ;—Granaries. Winnowing and Tea-drying Rooms, Carpenters' yards and sheds, and general depositories.

A gate on the south eastern corner leads to a water mill, in which the priests grind their flour, and to shops where Basket makers, Tailors, Shoemakers, and other artizans are employed—large plots of cultivated ground, fish ponds &c. affording satisfactory evidence that in enjoyment of the comforts of life both priests and attendant laymen are well versed. Not that the priests indulge in

any thing besides food of grain and vegetables;—
but these, in their modes of cookery, are well varied.
Maize flour porridge or rice, eaten with salt, and
vegetable soup, form the staples, accompanied by
greens, fresh or in partial decomposition, pickled
ginger, salad, beans, and grated bean curd, not unlike parmesan cheese both in taste and appearance.

In Sugar there appears to be little or no indulgence;—nor, excepting for the toast of the maize
porridge from the pan, do they seem to have much
relish for anything like Bread. Of liquids, Tea, and
the ptisan, *Tching-sha-yet*, mentioned at page 51,
are the principal indulgences;—no spirits—no opium—no tobacco, nor anything of an oleaginous
nature. As a rule they appear in excellent health
and spirits, and if, as has been stated, they are
burnt to death for infringment of the rules
of the institution — the principal of which are
abstinence from animal food and sensual indulgence—they do not appear to live in much dread
of the sword that hangs over them. Nor have they
need, as it is competent for any of these priests of
Buddha to give up their vocation and return to the
world as soon as they feel dissatisfaction with the
restraints imposed.

We might have supposed that in a service requir-
ing some asceticism, and the display of peculiar
talent to fit the superiors for the positions to which
they are elected by vote among themselves, attempts
would be made to elevate the order of the duties;—
we might have thought that learning or scientific
ability would be a qualification for higher posts.
—But it is not so; and, for all that is known
to the contrary, the Abbot of the largest Monastery
may be unable to write his own name, or do any
thing which the humblest of the brethren might not

be able to do. And yet they are not devoid of
ambition ;—marks of superiority among the fra-
ternity being shown in round spots on the caput
over the frontal bone, nine or twelve, three in a
row, about an inch apart, burnt in with an instru-
ment kept for the purpose.

To keep the head shaved is also a rule of the order,
and to wear robes of a peculiar kind, simple as
can be, loose and flowing, kept over the breast by
a large hook and ring. Excepting by his yellow
silk shoes, and it may be by a little cleaner dress, the
Abbot bears no insignia by which he may be known
from those below him;—and the best reason in the
world for keeping him to the proper performance
of his duties is the knowledge of the fact, that
those who have elected can also depose him. Reports of such arbitrariness, however, are not common.

Pilgrims to these Monasteries from distant lands
do very little themselves in the way of worship;—
The details are left to the priests, who have a fixed price of 1600 Cash for any kind of religious
service they may be called on to perform (20).
These services appear to consist of a repetition
of set forms of words, either in single voices or
in chaunts by a company of priests, sometimes
numbering as many as forty together—After a
series of chaunts, at the striking of a bell there
may be genuflexions for half an hour together,
the most ardent of the worshippers, and some of
them appear very sincere, striking the head on the
ground two and three times before they rise, to
wait, with hands uplifted in the attitude of prayer,
another tap of the bell and another call to send
them again prostrate. Some of the chaunts are
particularly pleasing ; but of the meanings of the

sounds uttered even the most learned in the land are ignorant—*Lo-way-la*—*Lo-way-la* on one note or varied half a note each way, is music pleasing enough to those fond of monotony,—changing after a quarter of an hour's repetition, perhaps, to *Too-way-woie*—*T o-way-woie*—or a more lively symphony of *Fau-sing-ko Ching-ko-way*—*Fau-sing-ko Ching-ko-waye* or some such words.

The Temple of the three goddesses at the *Choey-yen-size*, and the services performed in it, will be found highly pleasing to the quiet observer;—especially should the hour of service be near sunset, or before the break of day, when the subdued light from a couple of dozen of candles, all at an equal altitude about eight feet from the ground, and ranged in lines around the smokened hall, or at the altar piece, gives a peculiar mellow expression to the countenances of the performers, with their bald pates, and yellow or *more modest coloured vestments. Many of these priests are exceedingly sensible men, and on being asked why they pay adoration to images of wood and 'stone will reply that the spirit they address is one and the same with the Being worshipped by men of western lands;—but that western men, having more power of mind, are better able to realize the divinity than themselves and others of their countrymen, who require a visible representation of their god, else it is not in their power to confine their thoughts, and express their devotion with proper effect. As before stated, these priests, for the most part, are unlettered men, and, in nine cases out of ten, will inform the enquirer that their reason for becoming priests was a want of the means of existence. Occasion'ly, however, a child is born under the star of a particular spirit and, the parents

are directed by astrologers to devote the youth to
his service ;—an injunction to be evaded only by
the enlistment of a substitute—male or female. In
proportion to the male servers, the number of nuns
throughout the empire, is very inconsiderable (21).

Attached to the *Choey-yen-sze* are some 240
acres (1400 mow) of land, and in the value of the
timber on the domain, alone, the establishment is
rich. When spoken to of the rebellion going on
in adjacent provinces, and of the fears that must
be entertained for the continuance of their order, but
little from which an opinion can be formed is given
by the priests in reply;—they are passive on the
subject, and patiently await the coming of what, in
their opinion, appears to be inevitable—a rev olution
throughout the country. Conveniently blind though
they be, they are not so bigotted as to be ignorant
of the fact that the religion, or rather the mummery
they practise is entirely unworthy the light of
reason.

At the top of the gorge N.N.W. from the *Choey-
yen-sze* is another Monastery of thirty priests, a
building which, though no older in establishment
than the grander one below, is not particularly substantial in appearance, being constructed of wood
principally. On the way to it, and immediately in
the rear of the north wall of the *Choey-yen-sze*, is a
pleasant summer house ; and a quarter of an hour's
walk further on, on the left, is the small building or
Cremating house in which the bodies of deceased
priests are burnt to ashes. It is a small hexagon of
eight feet sides, and similar height, with a coved roof,
all built of brick, When Buddhism was practised
with more strictness then it now appears to be, the
legend runs that priests disobedient to the rules of
the order were burnt alive here ;—but such deeds
have not occurred within the present century.

Half an hour's walk from the Monastery, travelling in chairs is no longer possible for the male adult;—though small footed old ladies and unused-to-travelling Chinese teachers, with heads insensible to giddiness from the peculiar swinging motion imparted by the bearers to chairs when ascending heights, do manage to keep their seats without flinching. The first *Ding* from the commencement of the ascent is reached in about seven minutes, and eight minutes walking further on brings the traveller within view of the small temple at the entrance of the *Sze-tze-kow*, or Cave of the Lion's mouth. The strata at this height is of the red brown hard sand stone before spoken of. Few or no birds or animals are to be seen in this quarter; indeed, throughout the province, the brute creation is sparse ;—the necessities of the people, perhaps, inducing them to destroy and use for food all the *caro* crossing their path.

Seventeen minutes walking from the first brings the traveller to the second resting house, called the *Ping-sang-Ding*. In neither of these *Dings* are there idols, pictures, or tablets,—the vicinity of so much priestly sanctity being quiet sufficient for the native wayfarer apparently ;—*apropos* to the old English saying—"the nearer the Church the farther from the Divinity." Five minutes' walk from the second *Ding* are the quarters of a priest whose main occupation appears to be that of keeping the kettle or rather kettles boiling to supply passers by with warm tea. Here too can be obtained for a few cash, sweet cakes, dates, ground nuts &c.

The contrivance for keeping kettles away from or close to the fires, which are usually made of charcoal in large iron pans placed on trussels, is

most ingenious. A hollow bamboo, four or five feet
long, is suspended from the ceiling, and a rod with
a crooked end, on which hang the kettles, is placed
within it, and kept up or down by a small bamboo
spoon shaped stopper attached to the upper bamboo
by a string; the angling of this stopper, through
which the crook stick runs, having the effect of
keeping it at whatever altitude the cook wishes.

Chinese say that good tea can only be made with
the purest hill spring water; and here, at this little
cot, the purity of the water, which is led through a
hollow bamboo direct from the rill to the kitchen,
certainly produces a beverage such as connoisseurs
would pronounce exquisite. Some of the tea obtained at the way side dings is as different from the
tea *Europeen-ne* as can well be imagined. If an
Englishman's mode of giving it a similitude can be
realized,—it is the flavour, imaginary of course, of
"buttered cowslips." So proud are the Chinese of
their hill water tea, that throughout the country it
is not uncommon to see sign boards announcing
the fact that good " san suey " hill water, can be
had within;—in the same way that Tavern keepers at home advertise their Burton ale, Devonshire
cider, and Dublin stout.

It takes upwards of 20 minutes to walk from the
Tea *Ding,* or Temple as it should be called, there
being a small idol within it, to the point where the
road branches off to the S. W. ; and if, instead of
going on, the traveller sends on his chair to wait
for him at the top, and then himself proceeds along
this sou' western path, he reaches, in about seven
minutes, the very celebrated mausoleum of a priest
whose remains were interred beneath it so many
centuries ago that tradition is faulty with the
record. Here reside two priests, their cot or

perch being on such a narrow ledge that to reach the tomb the traveller has to pass through the house itself (22).

Since Dr. Medhurst's visit to this place in 1854, several Gentlemen from Shanghae have left their names in Indian ink on the external wall of the mausoleum. *

The rock here again, a grey granite, is quite different from the strata lower down. The mausoleum measures 13 feet 8 inches in diameter, and is built of square blocks of stone in a dome, the crown of which is about three feet above the spire of the tomb. The base of this tomb, a hexagon of two and three quarters feet wide sides, and three feet high, decorated with antique sculpture in relief, is constructed of the red sand stone spoken of, surmounted by a plastered cone, four feet high, and within which, it is presumed, is the honoured urn.—Pilgrims from afar immediately on reaching the entrance, or arch way, six feet high, prostrate themselves, and render as much homage as the most devoted Catholic would give to *Corpus-Christi.* The paved floor sounds hollow;—beneath it, perhaps, is another cave. Without the entrance is the following inscription 面目現在 (23).

Ten minutes walk from the mausoleum in an easterly direction, brings the traveller to the *Woh-mai-mew,* a Temple for the departed spirits of seven respected priests, for whom there are hexagonal columns 6 feet high, the centre one 7 feet, the

* Messrs. Butt and Coutts, and Aitcheson and Points, in May 1855, and Shaw and Francis in the June following. 1856 recorded no visitor there;—and in 1857 the writer was the first on record to approach it from the south.

tablets of the honored ones being locked up in
the plinths. Two or three minutes walk farther
on is another temple, with an idol in front of a tomb
as ancient as that just described. Some very
fine firs are to be seen here; one by the *Woh-mai-
mew*, at five feet above the soil, measuring 23½ feet
in girth, the spreading base covering space enough
to give a table-top ten feet square. A Plant in
this locality emits a peculiar gas-like scent, so
strong that it is unpleasant. Here among the
peaks, uninterrupted even by the chirp of birds, the
silence in a stilly day is most solemn, the rustle of
leaves and the silent dripping of water being the
only sounds.—Between the temple last mentioned
and a few minutes further walk to the monastery,
the traveller passes several monumental relics, and
will pause on the edge of some cliffs to take a com-
prehensive gaze at the scenery beneath; far in the
distance running a chain of mountains from E. by
N. to West by South apparently—the proportion of
valley to mountain seeming less than one to ten
—the *Choey-yen-sze,* in full proportion below, bearing S. S. E.

Three goddesses seated on lotus leaves are also
the favoured divinities at the upper *Teen-muh* sze,
or monastery on the western mountain; but after
seeing so much of Bhuddism at the grander establishment just left, there is no great attraction in the
services, and the traveller turns his observation to
the devotees, from great distances, continually arriving, resting for the night and then proceeding to one
or other of the more important shrines. These
pilgrims are generally dressed in new clothes, and
wear hats which foreigners in the south of China
are accustomed to call mandarin caps—but which,
in the north, decorated with a gilt button or other

wise, are worn on what may called state occasions
—such as worshipping at the tombs of ancestors,
on pilgrimages to temples, or other superstitious
performances.

A good walker can reach the top of the western
Teen-muh-san in about 50 minutes from the monastery; but it is a tiresome ascent, and, unless the
day is clear, hardly repays the labour it costs.
The ground sounds hollow to the feet,—the path
being laid with rough slabs of the hill strata.

On the top of the mountain is what is termed the
cave—a collection of large rocks on end, or across,
a-la Stonehenge.—One of these is a slab of about
12 feet long and five feet wide, length ways, and
resting on a rough upright, so forming a square
aperture not unlike a door way.—This is the cave.
From this point, about a mile and a quarter above
the Sea, the vallies below appear to diverge like
streams from a common centre (24).

After leaving the old Monastery the roughly laid
path takes up and away to the southward and westward—the huge mountain being literally skirted
round for a distance of about seven miles, when,
with the cave crowned peak bearing East, the
road runs down a precipitous flight of steps to
the N. N. W, ascending as sharply to an arched
Ding on a road side opposite. In some parts of the
road, before it branches off as descirbed, the side of
the mountain is so nearly perpendicular that travelling in a chair is out of the question to any one
keeping his eyes open. And here (singular circumstance for the province of Che-kiang,) the
hand of man has nought to do with the growth
of the straggling brush wood and wild grass, left to
luxuriate, die, and grow again without interference.
About five miles from the Monastery, at a point

where the mountain top bears about E.S.E., a path will be seen entering from the road, which, if followed, leads to the summit by an easier way apparently than that entering nearer the Monastery.

From the arched Ding to *Tai-ye-wan-ling*, the boundary of the Districts * Utsien* and *Haoufung* in *Che-Kiang*, and the border of *Ning-kwoh* in *Anwhuy*, the distance, up a tiresome ascent in a N. N.W. ly direction, is some five *lê*. From this point to *Ning-kwok-foo*, the chief city of the province of Anwhui, the distance is said to be 220 *le* westerly—the nearest Custom House Pass being *Tsien-suen-ling* (25).

PROVINCE OF ANWHUY

DEPARTMENT OF NING-KWOH.

From *Tai-ye-wan-ling* to *Tai-chew-fong-ling* the general course is about west; but the travelling is all mountainous, down one ascent and up another, through romantic glens and across barren hill sides, sharp pitches and no flag stones, for a distance of about eight miles. At the *Tai-cheu-fong-ling* the road breaks off from the direct course to the town of *Kwang-fuh-tze*, or *Kwang-fuzzy*, as it is called by the natives, and runs through some beautifully cultivated woodland country, along the ridges of hills towards *Le-san-yow*, a hamlet of forty five families. The Geologist has fine subject here for the study of the various stratæ;—first of what might be called yellow grey granite,—then lime stone rock—then again decomposed granite of a red brown colour ;—the hills being variously cultivated with bamboo, plum and fir trees, or maize, und the sedges whose leaves, are used in lining tea chests. The wood cutters sell a species

of beech nut, too, oily in the fruit, and as brown
as if exposed to the action of fire. But the road is
very narrow here, in some places not wider than a
man's foot, and generally impassable excepting on
dry sunny days.

From *Le-san-yow* to *Toong-haen* a large village
of 100 families on both sides of a valley, the distance
is about five *le* in a W.N.Wly. direction. There are
two taverns at *Toong-haen*, where travellers can
quarter;—and as there is no monastery, and no
priest, so there is no choice, and the best must be made
of the miserable-accomodations at command. The
valley here, running from W. S. W. to E. N.E. is
about a quarter of a mile across, and in beautiful cultivation;—but, unused to the sight of foreigners, and
at no great distance from the scene of active opera-
tions between the Rebels and Imperialists, the reception accorded to foreigners, at first, is mingled with
what appears to be distrust of his intentions. *

---

* Finding that enquiries regarding the fighting bands were
not palateable, they were not persisted in. The information
given, too, was most contradictory   By one it would be asserted
that Ning-kwoh foo was in the hands of the insurgents; by
another that it never had been in their possession ; by a third
that it had, but was evacuated. The last tale was afterwards found to be the true one. An Impérialist Soldier came to
Ningpo bringing from Ningkwoh foo certain of the Patriot Books
of religious doctrine, and in one of them was found the following
ode.—

> " Praise the Lord above, the great high Ruler,
> The really true holy Father of holy heaven,
> The Father of souls,
> The one only true God,
> The one only holy God,
>
> Praise the Celestial Elder Brother.
> The really true holy Saviour of the world
> The first born Son
> Who gave his life for men."

Praise the Celestial King,
The true-appointed, true and holy Lord of all nations,
The Governor T'hae-Ping.

Praise the Eastern King,
The holy Lord who redeems from sickness,
The true and holy Wind of God,
The true and holy Spirit.

Praise the Western King,
The holy Rain of God,
The true and honorable man of high heaven.

Praise the Southern King,
The holy Clouds of God,
The true and upright man of high heaven.

Praise the Northern King,
The holy Thunder of God,
The true and benevolent man of high heaven.

Praise the Assistant King,
The holy Lightning of God,
The true and righteous man of high heaven."

Remarking on this the translator writes,—
"The reader will observe that the five Kings here enumerated are designated respectively the *wind, rain, clouds, thunder,* and *lightning,* of God. This mode of classification is common among the Chinese. Thus they speak of the five elements, water, fire, wood, metal, and earth ; the five virtues, benevolence, uprightness, propriety, wisdom, and sincerity ; the five relations, of prince and minister, of father and son, of elder and younger brothers, of husband and wife, and of friend and friend ; the five colors, green, yellow, red, white, and black ; the five cardinal points, east, south, west, north, and centre, &c., &c. The number of their kings, as well as their names, *Eastern, Southern, Western,* and *Northern,* seem to have been suggested in this way, though there is a want of completeness in the fifth's not being designated *central.* But the designations of *wind rain, clouds. thunder,* and *lightning,* given to these kings are new, and seem to have been suggested by a misapprehension of the circumstance that, in the Christian books, from which they had derived so many of their ideas, the expression for the Holy Spirit is sometimes, " The Wind of God." Instead of understanding this expression as

synonymous with Spirit of God, or Holy Spirit, they seem to regard it as the *symbol* of this idea. Accordingly as they had been led to bestow upon the Eastern King, on account of his searching wisdom, extended influence and controlling power the title of Holy Spirit, which was symbolized by the *wind*, the idea was suggested of representing the virtues ascribed to his associates by the associated terms of *rain clouds thunder*, and *lightning*. This explanation may seem to some fanciful, but I have not been able to find a better one."

Warmly interested in the rebellion, and viewing, with regret, the general apathy in China regarding it, we take this opportunity to republish the Reverend Dr. Medhurst's—

CRITIQUE ON THE "IMPERIAL DECLARATION OF THAE-PING."

This pamphlet consist of two odes and two essays. The first entitled "an ode on the origin of virtue and the saving of the world." does not much answer to the name it bears. The first line, indeed, tells us that the origin of virtue is from Heaven, by which is meant God ; and then the author goes on to talk about virtue and God, in rather an unconnected strain ; but from beginning to end of the ode we hear nothing about the saving of the world, nor is the name or work of the Saviour once alluded to. We must ascribe something of this rambling forgetfulness to the fact of the author having to compose in rhyme, which has made him more attentive to the harmonical succession of sounds, than to the theme with which he professed to start. Notwithstanding, however, its want of connection. and the awkwardness with which the ode necessarily reads in a translation, there are many important truths, and some splendid passages to be met with therein, which in a great measure redeem its character.

In the commencement of the ode the author maintains the unity of God, who, he says, is the common parent of all, and to whom from the earliest ages down to a period approaching the Christian era, both princes and people gave special honor. On this he grounds the exhortation to all, to unite in worshipping him, from whom every fibre and thread, every drop and sop come, and to whom our daily devotions should be paid. To worship any other being, the author says, would be as vain, as it is sinful : he created all the elements of nature, every breath we draw depends on him, no other being can interfere with his arrangements, and to no one else can be ascribed the honour of our creation. Idols, it is affirmed, are only recent inventions ; creation, therefore, could not have originated with them. Growing eloquent in his pleadings for God, the author tells us, "He warms us by his sun, He moistens us by his rain, He moves the thunderbolt, He scatters the wind;" 'let us act, therefore, like honest men, and give to God the honour which is due to him alone.

The poet then proceededs to inveigh against lewdness, which he says calls down on those who practise it the wrath of Heaven, and brings with it its own punishment. He therefore exhorts his readers to immediate reformation, and refers them to the four prohibitions against improprieties, given out by a disciple of Confucius, who forbad the looking upon, the listening to, the talking about, or the imagining of any uncleanness.

His next exhortation is to filial piety, which he urges from the example of the inferior animals, saying that if we neglect this obvious duty, we show ourselves to be worse than the brutes. The poet then exhorts to the imitation of superior men, such as the great Shun, who moved Heaven by his filial piety; he reminds his readers of their obligations to their parents, which by their utmost effort they never can repay; and concludes by a motive of the strongest kind, saying, that in obeying our parents we shew our obedience to God

The 5th commandment having been disposed of, the writer proceeds to the 6th, and prohibits murder, on the ground that all men are brethren, and that their souls come alike from God, who views all mankind as his children; various examples are then given from Chinese history of the regard for human life, or the want of it, which was manifested by celebrated men, and of the recompense which followed it.

Offences against the 8th commandment then occupy the poet's attention, and theft is denounced as contrary to benevolence. After relating various instances of upright principle exhibited by the Chinese worthies of antiquity, the poet says, " From of old the honest and good have cultivated virtuous principles; riches and honours are but fleeting clouds, that cannot be depended on; if by killing one innocent person, or doing one act of unrighteousness, the ancient worthies could obtain empire, they would not allow themselves to practise it."

The poet then denounces witchcraft and magic arts; life and death, he says, are determined by Heaven, why then deceive people by the manufactures of charms; wizards and necromancers have always involved the world in poverty: the devil's agents have done service to devils, and the gates of hell stand open to receive them.

Gambling comes in for a share of the poet's reprobation: the vicious gamester, he says, conceals the dagger with which he. strikes his victim, therefore. we are to beware of a practice which is opposed to reason. The getting of unrighteous gain, he avers, is like quenching one's thirst with poison : the more you gamble the poorer you become.

Opium smoking is also condemned, upon which some people are so mad. In the present day, says our poet, many a noble son of Han has stabbed himself with the opium dagger. Wine has also ruined households, and rulers have perish d through their fondness for drink.

Some very excellent remarks follow, shewing the necessity of paying attention to the minutiæ of actions ; for, says our author, if you do not regard small matters, you will at length spoil great virtues.

The ode concludes by an appeal to the people, on the ground of the writer's having ascended to heaven ; on which account he says, his words are entitled to credence.

The second poetical piece is entitled " an ode of correctness," which is principally a play upon the word correct, that. term, either in its positive or negative form occurring 60 times. This poem contains various allusions to Chinese history, illustrative of the possession of correct principle, or the want of it. It may be interesting to a native reader, but it contains nothing worthy of notice by foreigners.

Then follow two prose productions, the first entitled, " An essay on the origin of virtue for the awakening of the age." It contains many truths liberal in their principle and new to the Chinese ; the sentences are somewhat tautological, to an extent that would not be tolerated in English composition, but the sentiments are congenial to every right feeling.

The writer begins by denouncing narrowness of mind, as exhibited in local likes and dislikes, and after ringing the changes on this subject throught a page or two, he proceeds to tell us that the ancient sages of China made no difference between one country and another, but viewed all alike. Having sufficiently illustrated these points, he tell us that God is the universal Father, that China and foreign nations are all equally under his rule and that all men are brethren.   After quoting a passage from Confucius, illustrative of a happy state of society, said to have prevailed in his days, the writer laments that " now, such a state of society is hardly to be looked for ; nevertheless when disorder is at its utmost height, order is sometimes elicited, and the unfeeling world is occasionally rendered loving."

The second prose production begins with the statement that all men have one origin, both as it regards their bodies, being

sprung from one ancestor ; and as it regards their souls, which
have all come from the original breath of God ; thus all under
heaven belong to one family, and should all regard each other as
brethen. The writer then goes on to combat the erroneous notion
current in China, that the king of Hades determined life and
death : this king of Hades, he says, is no other than the old ser-
pent, the Devil.* He then lays down a method by which men
may judge of the correctness of principles, and avers that those
which are diffused through all ages and countries are generally
right, while partial and private views are to be suspected : but the
principle above stated he adds is found neither in Chinese nor
foreign classics, but in the Buddhist and Taouist books an l therefore concludes that it must be wrong. This is not the first time,
he continues, that lies have been invented in China : for the ruler
of the Tsin dynasty imagined the existence of fairies ; Kwang-
woo, of the Han dynasty, sacrificed to the kitchen ; people of
later ages pretended that the dragon produced rain ; whereas rain,
it was evident came directly from heaven. Then we have some
references to the Old Testament, about the forty days rain in tne
time of Noah, causing the flood ; which rain was sent down by
God as a judgment upon a guilty world.† He goes on to say,
that a Buddhist book called the " pearly Record " also ascribes
the power of life and death to the king of Hades ; but the classics of China and foreign nations, he avers, all say that Heaven
produced and nourished every thing, and that life and death
are determined by fate, which is nothing else than the appoint-
ment of God. This appeal to foreign (by which is meant Christian) classics, as an authority in matters of faith, is a new thing
in China : as is also the allusion to the 審判 shin-pwan judgment. which God will enter into with the men of the world.

The writer goes on to state, that because men aspire after
longevity, and pant for good fortune, that therefore they are thus

* The phrase employed for expressing this latter idea is very similar to the
one used in Medhurst's and Gutzlaff's versions of the New Testament, as may
be seen by comparing them.

     Med's. & Gutz.'s vers.   *Insurgents' vers.*

     老蛇妖鬼   老蛇魔鬼

† The word used for " Old Testament " is the same as that employed by
Morrison and Gutzlaff. The name of Noah corresponds to that used by Gutzlaff,
viz: 挪亞 No-a, and not to Morrison and Afa, who employed 桜亞
No-a. In the mode of expressing the 40 days and 40 nights, the writer
agrees more with the Morrison than Gutzlaff. So that he must have had
both versions before him, or quoted by memory occasionally from one and
the other, as he happened to recollect.

prone to believe lies. Thus errors creep in, and get possession
of men's minds, and though God successively produces wise and
holy men, to convey the truth to others, they will not lend an
ear. Hence men, he says, are bewildered and ignorant of God,
they are also stouthearted and do not fear him. If their descen-
dants wish to get some knowledge of the truth, they do not know
where to obtain it. Then follow some beautiful and correct
statements regarding God, which we are tempted to exhibit in a
condensed form. " Taking a general view of the world, we
find that men though numerous are all created and supported by
God ; for every article of food and clothing they must depend on
God, who is the universal Father of all mankind. Life and
death, happiness and misery are all determined by him. When
I look up to heaven, I perceive that the sun and moon, stars
and planets, the thunder and rain, wind and clouds, are all the
wondrous effects of his mighty power : when I survey the earth,
I perceive that the hills and fountains, rivers and lakes, birds
and beasts, plants and fishes, are all the marvellous productions
of his mighty energies :" for this every man and women throughout the world, ought every morning to worship and every even-
ing to adore him.

The writer then meets an objection, that though God is to be
acknowledged as the sovereign of all, yet he must have various
ministers to aid him in protecting mankind. To which he answers, that should such exist, they must all be appointed by God :
but who ever heard of his appointing the idols which men are
in the habit of worshipping ? The writer continues, that God
did, at the creation, appoint angels ‡ to do his will ; and if so,
there is no need of idols, who are mere monstrosities, invested by
mortals, in defiance of his authority. The author then takes up
the same ground which a Christian missionary would assume in
arguing image-worship in the ten commandments. According
to the Old Testament, he says, God in former ages descended on
Mount Sinai, and gave forth the ten commandments, written
with his own hand on tables of stone ; and with an audible voice
commanded Moses, saying, 'I am the Lord God : thou shalt not
set up the image of any thing in heaven or earth, to bow down
to it and worship it ;' now your setting up images and worshipping them is a direct violation of the Divine command. §

---

‡ The word 神使 shin she, for angel, is after Morrison and Afa ;
Gutzlaff employs 天使 t'heen she.

§ The characters used for expressing Sinai, are 西奈 Se nae, which
are identical with those employed in Medhurst's and Gutzlaff's version of the

He further argues, that since God has forbidden the worship of images, these could not be employed in assisting him in protecting mankind : and if God could make the world without their aid, he could surely preserve the world in existence without any assistance. The writer then states, in a way peculiarly Chinese, that God has made the ground on which we stand, and the food we eat ; he also gives us sun and rain ; deprived of his aid, we could not live a single moment; why then should we pray to idols?

He then supposes an objector saying, ' but my idol is efficacious.' And says, in reply, that all our blessings come from the great God, while men erroneously suppose that they come from some corrupt devil. The associating with such, he continues, is not only an outrage against Heaven, but an offence against natural conscience, showing that the persons so acting are rebellious both against reason and religion. He then inculcates the duty of praying to the universal Father ; and brings forward the promise of the Saviour, as an encouragement to its performance : quoting the well known passage contained in Matthew 7 : 7. "ask and it shall be given you," &c. It is worthy of observation, that in this quotation, the writer has copied almost exactly the version of Medhurst and Gutzlaff, published in 1835, the resemblances being nearly identical, as follows :—

Med. & Gutz. vers.	*Insurgents.' vers.*
扣尋求 門則則 則遇得 開著之	扣尋求 門則則 則遇得 開之之

After having exhorted his readers to pray to our heavenly Father, he points out the folly of addressing such applications to idols, quoting from Psalms 115 : 5, in which he imitates, in some degree, both Morrison's and Gutzlaff's version, with only a little transposition and omission, resulting probably from his having quoted from memory.

The writer then goes on to point out the way in which idolatry sprang up in China. From the earliest antiquity, he says,

New Testament: while in Morrison's former edition, and Gutzlaff's more recent edition of the Old Testament, 西乃 Se-nae are employed. The word used for *written* 緒 shen, is found in Gutzlaff's, but in none other of the former versions. The phrase "I am the Lord God," is very similar to the one employed by Gutzlaff.

down to the close of the three dynasties (B. C. 220) both princes
and people generally worshipped God. Some innovations had,
however, sprung up two thousand years previously, when the
Kew Le believed in evil spirits, and corrupted the tribes of Mea-
ou, who are accounted the aborigines of China. ‖ Corruptions
had crept in, also, about a thousand years afterwards, when men
were employed to represent the ghost of the departed ; but during
all this period, according to this writer, the mass of the people
continued to be monotheists, as at the first. As we approach the
Christian era, a superstitious regard for ghosts and hobgoblins
increased, and the sea was looked to as the abode of the genii.
This led to an interference with the previous monotheistic practice, and one of the rulers of the Han dynasty erred egregi-
ously, in supposing that the four quarters with the centre of the
world were each under the dominion of a separate Deity. Corruptions speedily increased, and soon after the rise of the Christian
era, the emperor Ming, hearing that a holy man had arisen in
the west, sent men to look for him, who instead of penetrating
to Judea, stopped short at India, from whence they introduced
the religion of Buddha, with its numerous images and superstitious rites. The founder of the Taou sect, also, came in for his
share of religious honours and one of the emperors thence gave
himself up to be a priest in one of the monasteries, from whence
his ministers had to redeem him, at a large sum. Things went on.

‖ The circumstance here alluded to is detailed in the Shoo-king, when
"Shun directed his officers to cut off the connection between earth and
heaven, and prevent the pretended descent of spirits." The Commentators
say " that having been subject to oppression, the people, ignorant of its cause,
had recourse to spirits, and sacrificed to demons. From this arose marvellous
and lying stories, and men lapsed into error. According to the records of
the country it appears, that in the decline of Shaou-haou's reign, the Kew Le
threw the constant virtues into confusion, and thus men and spirits were
mingled together ; every family had its conjuror, and the people made
profane use of sacrificial implements. In consequence of this men and spirits
were thrown into confusion. History declares, that when a country is about
to flourish, attention is paid to the people, and when it is about to perish, attention is paid to the spirits. On this account Shun prohibited the people
from using magical arts in order to bring down the spirits. One says, that in
a well-regulated age, spirits and elves do not appear, and people do not pray
to the spirits ; but in times of confusion people are much given up to spirits
and elves they talk of necromancy and fortune telling without end. The
officers of Shun displayed the principles of enlightened virtue, that men might
avoid being perverted by idle and superstitious fancies, and no longer seek for
happiness from spirits. For men are apt to err from correct principles when
they become deluded by spiritual beings ; but when they attend to the inva-
riable principles of goodness, they seek for happiness in the way of constant
virtue, and not in that of monstrous appearances." In the above remarks of
the commentators, wherever the expression *spirit, sprite,* or *spiritual being*
occurs, the word in the original is *Shin.*

from bad to worse, according to our author, when Hwuy, one of
the emperors of the Sung dynasty, changed the name which had
been used for God into one used to designate an imaginary deity.
This alteration of the venerable name of God is looked upon by
our author as displaying a great want of reverence towards him, ¶
and he proceeds to trace the subesquent misfortunes which came
upon the emperor Hwuy, and his son, to this source. In consequence of all these corruptions having crept in, our author says
it is not to be wondered at that the Chinese should be now so
ignorant of God, and destitute of his fear.

Some reformers, he says, have occasionally sprung up, but the
remedies applied were only partial : though idolatry was in some
instances put down, in the majority of cases it was allowed to go
on. Whereas, according to him, all these genii and fairies,
superhuman and monstrous appearances, together with these im-
pure rites and forbidden sacrifices, should have been discontinu-
ed ; on the ground that besides the great God there is no spirit
entitled to such honour as the Chinese have been accustomed to
pay them.** All the images of wood and stone, which have
been set up to represent these imaginary beings, are mere inventions of men, otherwise intelligent, who have allowed themselves

---

¶ This change in the name of God, which excites so much the wrath of
our author, is simply an alteration from the usual form *Shang-te* into *Yuh-te* :
the former designation had been the name which was applied to God by the
Chinese from time immemorial, and the latter was a name invented by the
Taou sect, and used several hundred years before the time of Hwuy to
designate an idol. After having spoken of changing the appellation, *ching*, or
the great God our author, in recurring to the subject, and in order to show his
reverence for the Deity, says, that his honourable name (tsun haou) was
changed. The phrase *tsun haou* in certain connections may perhaps be rendered a title of honour. But here the meaning evidently is "honorable name."
We have a similar expression in the Three Character Classic of the Insurgents, where the phrase is inverted, but conveys the same meaning ; "*haou
tsun tsung,* his name is most honourable." It is not correct therefore to say,
that the insurgents have indicated the fact that they use *Hwang Shang-te*
as a title of honour. They have indicated no such fact : but they have used
Hwang Shang-te, Shang-te and Te, precisely in the same way in which we
use the word God. In Gutzlaff's version of Genesis, a portion of which they
have reprinted, Shang-te is used as a translation of Elohim ; in their version
of the ten commandments, the insurgents have employed the same term where
Elohim stands in the original ; and no one, who had not some fond theory to
carry out, would ever dream of the insurgents having used Shang-te in those
cases as a title of honour.

** It is evident, from the context, that the writer by the word *spirit* here,
means such spiritual beings as men have been in the habit of worshipping, but
which he thinks are not entitled to that honour. That he could not mean to
say, besides the great God there is no spiritual being, is plain, because he uses
the word *shin* to designate not only the genii which have no real existence,
but the spirits of men which have.

to be deluded by the devil. The true spirit, he continues, is God; but those images which men are in the habit of worshipping represent only devils, the mass of whom consists of nameless noxious inventions, such as the spirits thought to preside over the various quarters of the world, and the myrmidons of the king of Hades. Having denounced these pretended spirits, he says most truly, the great God, (Hwang Shang-te) he is the God, ('Te) and he alone is entitled to that appellation. Through a want of acquaintance with the Christian Scriptures, and certainly not with the view of sympathizing with the deniers of our Lord's divinity, with whom he never could have come in contact, the author of the pamphlet before us, says, "that even Jesus, the first-born son of God, is only called our Lord, and is not called God;" who then he asks would dare to assume the designation of God? would he not for his blasphemous assumption be speedily consigned to hell He therefore exhorts his readers to worship God alone, and thus they will become his sons and daughters here, and obtain his blessing hereafter.

In closing our critique on this pamphlet, we shall, once for all, refer to the *practice* of the insurgents with regard to the word used for God. Having compared all the books printed by them, and brought by the *Hermes* from Nanking, we have drawn up the following list of the number of instances in which they have used words bearing any affinity to Shang-te, and T'heen for God; as contrasted with those in which they have employed Shin for God, or gods. We have also adduced the instances in which other terms are employed to designate the Lord of all, besides those that have any relation to either Shang-te or Shin; and we close our list by showing in how many cases the word Shin is used for angel, genii, and spirits.

I.—Instances in which Shang-te and its cognates have been used for God.—

			Times.
Shang-te used for God by way of eminence, sometimes accompanied with the statement that Shang-te is one, and that there is no other Shang-te but this one, - - - - - - - - - - -			175
Hwang Shang-te	do	do.	371
Te	do.	do.	17
T'heen-te	do.	do.	2
T'heen	do.	do.	100
T'heen-foo	do.	do.	194
Hwang-t'heen	do.	do.	2

Hwang-t'heen Shang-te do. do. 1
Haou-t'heen do. do. 2
T'heen-kung do. do. 1
——— 865

II.—Instances in which Shin is used for God, or gods :—
Shin used for God, or the Supreme Spirit, - - - 4
Shin used for others besides the Supreme, - - - 2
Chin shin, for the true God, or Spirit, - - - - - 18
Seay-shin, for depraved gods, or spirits, - - - - 14
——— 38

III.— Cases in which other terms are employed for the Lord of all :—
Shang-choo, used for Lord, - - - - - - - - - - 52
Choo-tsae do. - - - - - - - - - - 2
Jehovah, - - - - - - - - - - - - - - - - - 1
Hwa-kung, creator, - - - - - - - - - - - - - 1
——— 56

IV.—Cases in which Shin is used for spirit, or enters into composition to express angel, genii, &c. :—
Shin, used for the Spirit of God, - - - - - - - 2
Shing Shin fung, Holy Spirit, in which Shing, stands for holy, and Shin-fung for spirit, - - - 4
Tsing-shin for animal spirit, - - - - - - - - - 2
——— 8

Shin-tseib, traces of spiritual beings, used in the sense of miracles, - - - - - - - - - - - 4
Shin-seen, genii, - - - - - - - - - - - - - - 8
Shin-she angels - - - - - - - - - - - - - - 6
Shin-chow, region of spirits, name for China in opposition to Kwei-fang, land of devils, used for Tartary, - - - - - - - - - - - - 4
Shin-yay, spiritual father, coupled with Hwan-foo, ghostly father, - - - - - - - - - - 3
——— 33

We have observed elsewhere, that the example of the insurgents is of little value as philological argument, because they borrowed their religious terms, as they did their views of doctrine, mainly from the foreigners who preceded them. Their *practice*, however, shows to what class of terms they felt most inclined ; and from this we find that they employed Shang-te and its cognates for God by way of eminence, in almost every instance. This is indeed the *rule* observed in their books, while the use of him, in the same sense, is the *exception*.

W.H.M.

From *Toong-haen* to *Koo-he-qui-show*, a small hamlet in a north-easterly direction the distance is about four miles. Before reaching this hamlet, however, the traveller crosses from the *Anwhui* into the *Chekiang* province again, by the *Koon-foo-kwan*, or Confucian pass—a gorge about sixty yards across, with a broad military causeway, thirty feet wide, having, on one side, a granite built arched gateway, through which, with determined soldiers for its maintenance, a passage could not easily be forced (26). For good distances each side of the pass the valley is narrow and capable of affording tentage accomodation for as many troops as would be requisite either in defence or assault. On the *An-whuy* side of the pass is a small temple dedicated to Confucius, and, rarely seen, a small gilt image of the honoured Sage, to which homage is paid as to a god.

PROVINCE OF KIANG-SIU

DEPARTMENT OF HOO-CHOW.

A short distance from *Koo-hoo-qui-show* is *Wei-zhong* a hamlet of 100 families, and some two or three miles further on is *Pek-ling-wo*, a little distance from *Choong-ching* a hamlet of 90 families. Lime stone is the formation here, the rock out of which the path way is cut being as black and glossy as coal.

Timber is transported in raft in large quantities from this region;—poles such as would be used for scaffolding, being sold at the stream's edge for as low a rate as 50 cash a pecul—say two pence per hundred weight! Salt, the article brought in barter for the wood, costs, duty paid, 70 cash a catty—say three pence per pound !

From *Choong-ching* to *Kow-jow*, where, as the name implies, there is a high bridge, (curved granite slabs) of very good workmanship, the distance, in a north-easterly direction, is over five *lĕ*, and from *Kow-jow* to *Chong-chuen* a village of 200 families it is also five *lĕ*. But there is no need for giving the particular course from village to village on the route from the Confucian pass to *Haou-foong-yuen*, the chief city of the district entered on after leaving the Province of *Anwhuy*, the general direction being about E. N. E.—for the most part over paved roads and a level country, and by the beds of streams increasing in size as they progress from their sources around the *Teen-muh-san*.

From *Chong-chuen* to *Toh-san*, a village of 150 families, the distance due East is 5 *lĕ*—*Amoo* a village of 100 families being a little way beyond it. But these villages, and those of *Cow-ka-hai* of 150 families, *Cheong-le* of 80 families, *Mo-sah* of 50 families, and *Tong-chin* of 100 families, are all at little distances from each other. In a N.N.Wly direction from *Cow-ka-hai*, distant about five miles, is a curious finger shaped rock, standing erect and apart from the mountain adjacent. The ladies in this quarter wear pretty red serge gaiters, the serge being almost the only specimen of European manufacture to be seen in this part of the interior. Approaching *Seen-hing-ling-sze*, the quarters of two or three priests, an artist, with time for the work, will find a most interesting picture—Cliffs, cottages, pagodas and streams in sweet variety— and, if required, a room for a day or two without much incovenience to the *Hozhangs* (priests).

Foong-sa-ven and *Low-chee*—the latter a village

of a hundred families, the other the residence of two
or three only, are but little distances beyond *Tong*
chin. Tea Bushes are again seen in this locality,
and proceeding onwards over a wide ford, and,
through a walled lane, for about five *lĕ*, the traveller arrives at a shrine to the Dragon God, close by
which, in the grove by itself, is a small permanent
Theatre of varnished wood.   At *Low-zhak-kong*
a village of 300 families, the country takes quite
a level appearance, the hills each side becoming
smaller and smaller as though they formed the end
of a huge chain (27)—*Leang-zak-you* of some 20
families, *Toong-djean* of 1000, and *Yah-kong-djow*
by a plank and trussel bridge of 21 apertures—say
250 feet long—are all at no great distance from
the *Low-zhak-kong* mentioned.—The Strata in this
quarter is of a blue black slate.

From *Yah-kong-jow* to *Sac-wan-lee*, a hamlet
of 20 families, the distance, over eight *lĕ*, runs
through a fine wood land, quite different from any
thing the other side of the mountain range.

Some time before reaching *Sac-wan-le* a seven
storied Pagoda S.E. of the city of Haoufoong meets
the view; and in the suburbs of the city are the
best quarters for the foreign traveller (poor enough)
at the *Kwan-ti-mew*, or Temple of the God of War.

Haou-foong, or *Shaou-foong-yuĕn* is a poor
apology for a walled city,—the walls, about a mile
and a half round, being in some places broken away
wide enough for a carriage and pair to be driven
through.   It was a decent place enough once, perhaps, and the city Temple on a level with the top
of the south wall is a fine building.   The shops in
the western suburbs, however, far surpass those
within; but it is a poor place for business, this being
inferred from the want of silver in negotiations;—

Money changers having the conscience to offer 600
cash only for the most beautiful Carolus dollar
ever handled—800 cash in barter for Rice being an
exteme price (28).

There is a junction of two wide though shallow
streams on the S.E. angle of the city, a well pebbled road from the north gate leading by a large
parade ground to a long plank and trussel Bridge,
which the traveller crosses to the stream's right
bank —The low ground hereabout is profusely
studded with mulberry trees—Firs and elms, in
clumps here and there, varying the scene.

About four miles N.E. from *Haou-foong* is *Yah-
chong* a small village—and Eight *le* further on
Tow-foo, a busy little place of 200 families. The
river appears deep here, and there is a good deal of
traffic by bamboo rafts and boats of shallow draft;
—but the average depth is but little over three feet,
as found at a ferry a little further on. A short distance from *Tong-foo* is *Tow-foo* and north of that
Sze-Dong—E. N. E., again being the small hamlet
of *Se-tche-sah.* Here the river is crossed in ferry
boats from the *Haou-foong* to the *Gnan-keih,* or
as it is locally pronounced *Ane-chee* District,—the
first small village on the *Ane-chee* side being *Che-
che-sah,* a small place in a grove near fields of tea
bushes over wheat.

Chu-ko-lo of two or three houses is N.E. about one
mile from *Che-che-sah*—and a little further on *Ho-
foo-loong* of similar size. *Ing-ka-loong* is the
next village, and after that *Sac-a-san,* both of them
exhibiting a good many tidy looking houses—the
winding streams among the wood land giving a
picturesque character to the route—the flat slab-
bed and pebbled path way being in excellent condition. From *Sac-a-san* to a Ding a short distance

from *San-qua-lee* the road takes a sharpish ascent
for a little distance over steps cut out of the rock.
San-qua-lee is a village of 150 families about 10 *le*
from *Chung-chow-chune*, a hamlet in the suburbs
of the district city of *Ane-chee.*

Ane-chee is not much larger than *Haou-foong*,
but the walls are in better condition, and there are
no such wide gaps in them as those told of.
The gates are small, not over seven feet square, the
houses built principally of wood.   But more than
half the enclosure is covered with mulberry trees
and large pools of water; and the traveller feels
repeatedly induced to put the question—"What on
earth can be the use of these walled cities ?" Carolus dollars change for 950 cash here, and ten cash
pieces are current.

On the East side, the city is skirted by the
River bed, and beyond the river is a pretty little
Pagoda low down among some Shrubbery.   A
moat runs round the city on the sides not protected
by the river ;—a well constructed arched Bridge by
the south gate leading into the suburbs, about the
best part of the place as usual.   The North wall has
recently been repaired, and looks quite formid able
to travellers approaching in that direction.   Only
four villages are met between *Ane-chee* and *Mai-
chee*, a distance of about eight miles, viz *Kwong-
heen-kong-deo—Zan-woo-Ding—Show-koon* and
Kow-jow-Deo.

At *Zan-woo* five miles from *Maichee*, Canals
lead off from the main stream, and run up in a N.Wly
direction to the *Tae-hoo*, or great Lake, and boats
can be hired here to take the traveller on there if
he wishes. *Mai-chee*, though called a village only,
appears to be a place of considerable traffic, and
two Government functionaries, one of them a Mili-

tary, one a Civil officer have their quarters here (29).
There are upwards of 1,000 families in the place,
and there must be a large migratory population of
raft men from the hills, and boat men engaged in the
Hoo-chow Trade. From *Mai-chee* to the Ferry at
which Boats can be obtained for the passage to Hoo-
chow, the distance is about seven *lē*—the head boat
man of the place being of the family name of Tong
(*Tong-Seen-sang*).

The distance from Mai-chee Ferry to Hoo-chow
is said to be 90 *lē*. It is in excess of this, but the channel, from 50 to 200 feet wide, winds a good deal—
S.S.E.—E.S E.—N.E.—E S. E.—S. E. E.N.E. and
East, all being noted within a three hours' run, the
general direction being due East. Thirty *lē* from
Hoo-chow is *Yuen-tong-jow*—Ten *lē* east of which
is *Ne-cha-veng*—and as far farther on, *Yah-co-
chaong*; the ground on both sides, a continued level,
being cultivated in the proper season with Indian
wheat;—Mulberry trees luxuriating in all directions.

At Hoo-chow the stream deepens, and Junks of
three and four hundred tons burthen discharge
their cargoes close to the banks.—But though of
such tonnage, these vessels are flat bottomed, and do
not draw at the outside more then six feet of water.

Hoo-chow, the *Foo* or Chief city of the department, is a place of considerable importance, and
judging from the busy habits of the people, no doubt
a desirable abode. It is from Hoo-chow that much
of the Silk for the Shanghae market is taken,
though little of the manufacture of it within the
walls is seen. Wide and deep canals run through
the city, crossed in various places by handsome and
capacious bridges. The walls, which are in very
excellent condition, 30 feet wide and 20 feet high,
are upwards of six miles in circuit, and from the

numbering and allotment. of the lofty battlements
into sections, it does not appear likely that the place
would be found unpreparcd should a visit be paid
to it by the expected rebels. Hills on the south of
the city are crowned with defensible barracks; and
whilst these remained in the hands of the city's hol-
ders would prevent successful assault in that direction. On the other hand, if in the possession of
assailants, attempt at defence would be unavailing;
A lofty seven storied Pagodá on a hill south of the
city commands, in a clear day, a view of the Tae-
hoo, or great Lake. and the country adjacent. Very
much of the interior of the City is unbuilt on, or
appropriated for archery grounds.—An avenue near
the south gate is lined with upwards of a dozen
Memorial columns, of finished antique workmanship

At Hoo-chow and the country near are manufactories of the Japan varnish used in the south. A
knowledge of this preparation would be prized in
Europe, and, with time and opportunity, a skilful
inquirer might obtain some useful infor mation regarding it. The preparation, whatever it is, is
wrung out in cloths by men working near a slow
fire. Rice, still the chief article of food among
the people, is dear here—viz, from 5,800 to 5,000
cash a pecul, or at Shanghae currency a little short
of three pence a pound.

Hoochow stands partly on the *Ané-chĕ* (*Gnan-
keih*) District, partly on the District of *Wu-Dzing*
(30) and after leaving by the Canal, the route to
Pahledeo, three or four miles from the eastern
walls is about E. by S.—Two miles or so East of
Pahledeo is *Sing-sang* and about a mile further
Yah-jong-kok.

From this point to *Shou-ming fu*, a distance of

ten miles E. by N.—the canal runs by the villages
of *Tching za—San-quon-deo, Chang-teng* and
Yat-ling-jow—the low hills around being thickly
studded with Firs or Mulberry trees, over Wheat,
Beans and Grassicher.—Bridges of excellent workmanship are met at various points where the
streams go north or south from the principal
Channel A little way beyond *Yatling-jow* is the
Poo-dee-mew; from which *Nan-Dzing* or *Noan-
zin,* and unwalled town of 40 or 50,000 inhabitants
bears N. E. distant about 3 miles. *Nan-Dzing* is
a very busy place, giving employment to many
coopers of the lacquered tubs and implements sold
in northern China markets, and occasionally seen in
the south.

Jin-zek, another large town on the Canal's
banks, is about five miles from *Nan-Dzing*; and
half a dozen miles further on, in a North easterly
direction, is *Say-chee,* also a place of considerable
size. The next place of note, after passing *Say-
chee,* and about Three miles east of it is *Ping-bong.*
This is a very interesting place, the principal trade
being in oil and oil cake of which there are several
manufactories.   By the Eastern entrance is a
pretty Temple (*Kwei-shin-kwok*) with a shrine
to *Te-chang-wan* the Goddess of Earth—the view
from the top of the Pagoda to the southward
and westward being over lagoons and streams for
immense distances—Northward and eastward the
country is flat for miles, and cultivated with the yellow flowered grassicher spoken of and with beans;
—and in a Lake close by, there is a picturesque
temple on a small islet called *Jow-bing-boo-doe.*
Eastward runs the Canal to Shanghae. At the
entrance of the temple beneath the Pagoda, the
unbeliever in the virtue of Buddhism feels a strong

inclination to laugh at the very jolly appearance
of an idol, the whole of whose body is hidden but
the face, which peers through a round aperture at
its devotees, speaking as plainly as inanimation
can speak—"What fools you are to think I can do
any good for you!" Only two priests are attached
to this temple;—a censer in the Court bearing date
the 52d year of the Emperor *Kang-he,* so leading
to the inference that that was the period when the
establishment was created.

The process of manufacturing Oil cake, and
obtaining the Oil is as follows. Beans, *Calavan-
cas,* the common white bean of commerce, are
first thrown into a shot. Leading, in small quantities, as permitted by a crank worked by a cog
wheel, down to a large flat stone, on which two
very heavy rollers are moved by blinkered water
bullocks. So macerated under the rollers, the
meal is removed to another shoot leading to a pair
of fluted mill stones, and thence thrown into a bin
by which is a furnace and two small boilers.
These boilers have apertures on their tops, through
which the quickly generated steam is permitted
to escape into wicker topped recesses of small
half peck measures of an oval shape. In these
wicker tops are placed the Bean meal, and five
seconds' passage of the steam through them is quite
sufficient to convert the meal into cakes. Speedy as
thought these cakes are then transferred from the
forms to twisted rattan hoops,—of similar shape,
then covered with thin grass, and, in a pile of some
two dozen at a time, transported to a square
horizontal frame, where they are compressed by
wedges until the oil exudes into a tank beneath.
So pressed, the cakes are again moved, stripped
of their grassy wrap pings, placed in piles to dry,

afterwards wrapped in straw, and, finally, sold as required. Either as manure for the ground, or food for cattle, these bean cakes are much coveted (31).

DEPARTMENT OF KIA-HING.

A short distance East of *Ping-bong* is *Hing-wong* ; and between that and the hamlet of *Sow-Dee*, twenty miles or so further east, the traveller passes the villages of *Sah-ca-coong, Tah-sean-wo See-cheng,—Loo-fae,* or *Loo-chae* (a place of 1,200 families) and *Jow-woo-sah.*

The black slime from the stream bed takes the place of manure in this quarter. The mode of obtaining it is ingenious. To the end of a stout bamboo a piece of concave wicker work is attached—a similar piece of wicker work being so fixed that when the stout bamboo thrust on the bottom has taken out a scoop of the mud, by the pressure downwards of a lighter bamboo the wicker concave collapses like a clamp shell, and confines the slime until it reaches the surface, when, by pinching together the light and stout bamboos, as we would a pair of tongs, the clamp opens, and the contents are emptied into a boat, whence, along side the bank, it is transferred to the shore, by means of a basket swung with ropes through the sides, by two men one at each end of the boat.

Ching-zeh is large town three or four miles N.E. of the hamlet of *Sow-dee* spoken of, and here may be seen, in quantity, the bamboo articles of furniture sold at the Consular ports and about the northern country—such as chairs, stools, baskets, lamp-stands &c. Bread is not to be obtained at this town—but plenty of bean " fixins" such as

curd cakes, smoked twist &c., are exposed in the
stalls. Tobacco is grown and cut, too, here. On
the whole there is a quiet air of business in the
streets, speaking great things for the thriftiness and
content of the inhabitants.

Eight or Nine miles N. E. of *Ching-zeh* is *Sam-
pah-dong*, a batch of red coloured houses on an is
let in a lake ; a lofty lamp post serving to render
it the light house for some miles around. Five
or six miles further on is a fine town called *Che-
ka-kwok*. Though not formally walled, the houses
have lofty backs, and join together, so that it is
not possible to get into the streets excepting by
guarded ways. The great feature of the place is a
splendid five arched granite Bridge—the centre
arch being over 35 feet in span.

PROVINCE OF KIANG-SU.

DEPARTMENT OF SUNG-KIANG.

Tsing-poo-yuen (or *Tching-koo-yuen* as it is called by the inhabitants,) the chief city of the district,
is about 5 miles N E. of *Che-ka-kwok*. It is another of the 1,600 walled establishments, and though
small is a neat place—The walls, brick over stone,
are in very good condition, and are entered at the
north and west sides direct from the water—there
being hardly room for a coffin between the wall
and the stream.

S. S. E. from *Tsing-poo* stands a pagoda on a
high mountain (Sing kong?) and a short distance
from the somewhat extensive suburbs on the N. E.
at *Tching-mo-deo*, is the *Tai-ping* Granary, a

series of six rows of white washed barrack like
buildings, five hundred feet long, capable of containing an immense quantity of grain (32).

From the Provincial Granary the canal takes a
winding direction—Westerly, northerly, easterly
and southerly—but on the average about N.E.—(33)

Only two villages remain to be noted, *viz Poon-
zan-keo* and *Pan-hok-quong*—the country being
ornamented with trees, not all planted, apparently,
for cutting down purposes. Excepting a Ferry
called *Ching-ka-chong,* about 15 miles from Shang
hae, no other village finds a place in our register.

APPENDIX.

NOTES.

—

1.—Page 2.—This is a variety of the *Brassica Napus*, and is thus spoken of by Fortune in his first volume of "Wanderings."—

"The oil plant, *Brassica Chinensis*, is in seed and ready to be taken from the ground in the beginning of May. This plant is extensively grown in this part of China, both in the province of Chekiang and also in Kiangsoo,. and there is a great demand for the oil which is pressed from its seeds. For the information of readers not acquainted with botany, I may state that this plant is a species of cabbage, producing flower stems three or four feet high, with yellow flowers, and long pods of seed like all the cabbage tribe. In April, when the fields are in bloom, the whole country seems tinged with gold, and the fragrance which fills the air, particularly after an April shower. is delightful.
*   *   *   *   *

"Very large quantities of the cabbage tribe are cultivated for the sake of the oil which is extracted from their seeds. They are planted out in the fields in autumn, and their seeds are ripe in April and May, in time to be removed from the land before the rice crops. It must not be supposed, however, that the whole of the land is regularly cropt in this manner, and that, as some writers inform us, it never for a moment lies idle, for such is not the case."

To this may be added that the boat people of Kiangsoo appear to live almost entirely on the young sprouts, a delicious oleaginous vegetable ; but almost too powerful for an European traveller's food.

2.—Page 2.—Dr Macgowan, our fellow travel-ler, the highest botanical authority in this part of world, has kindly furnished the following informa-tion regarding this *Peo-moo,* or *Pei-mü* bulb, as gathered from the Chinese Pharmacopœia and his own experience.—

" Its name is derived from its resemblance to a cowrie, a shell which was used for money in China until about the third century of our era. Two kinds are in use,—one from the province of Sze-chuen, the other the product of the mountainous parts of the department of Ningpo. The former are the size of the smallest cowries; white, of farinacous fracture, and slightly bitter :—the latter is half as large again, and of brownish color. It is recommended in a host of complaints; but used chiefly in those of the air stoppages. It is of undoubted utility in coughs, promoting expectoration, and uniting demulcent with tonic properties. I am aiming to introduce its culture, and also its medical use into the West.

"As you need a popular, not a professional charac-ter of the *Pei-mu* (*Cowrie Mother*) I may men-tion an instance of its external employment—for it is often applied in surgical cases.—A merchant who lived during the period of the Tong dynasty had an ulcerated tumor on his left arm, just be-

low the shoulders, which resembled the human face.
It gave him no pain,and his general health was
good One day he playfully poured a drop of wine
into the thirsty looking mouth of his left hand
man ; — whereupon the ulcer face reddened and
swelled. He then tried it with various eatables,
and found that when he fed the tumor it ex-
panded, and when the supplies were stopped it
settled down. At the recommendation of a celebrated doctor he administered all sorts of medicines to
the omniverous tumor, mineral, vegetable and animal. Nothing made any difference with it until he
gave it some *Pei-mu*.—Pleased with its action, he
thrust a culm of mat grass into the mouth, and
through that tube introduced an infusion of the
root. In a little while the brows fell off, the eyes
closed and shrivelled up, and so did the mouth, and,
after a short time, the image was effaced entirely.
Our author in detailing the case, which must not be
taken as a sample of Chinese medical writing, says
he is really unable to tell what disease that was;—
nor can I."

3— Page 2.—As stated further on,—Measures
of all kinds vary in different districts, and time did
not afford us an opportunity of testing the content
of a *Ching* in Fungwha. According to the table
of capacities furnished by Gutzlaff in his "China
opened" Chapter XIV;—a *shing* equals 31½ cubic
punts—a punt being the tenth part of a Chinese
covid. This would give the content of a shing
(ching and shing being identical we presume) at
a little under three quarters of an English pint.
Gutzlaff says.—
The measure of contents, which is seldom used, nearly every

article, and even fire-wood being weighed, are the following :—
6 Suh make a Kwei, 10 Kwei a Chaou, 10 Chaou a Tsuy,
—The table in "Chinese opened," referred to is follows—
10 Tsuy a Chŏ, 10 Chŏ a Hŏ, 10 Hŏ a Shing, or 31½ cubic
punts, 10 Shing a Tow, 316 cubic punts, 5 Tow 1 Hwŏ, 1,580
punts, and 2 Hwo a Shih, or 3,160 cubic punts. These however are only used in government accounts; the common peop'e
avail themselves of the following— 2 Yŏ make a Hŏ, 10 Hŏ make
a Shing or pint, 10 Shing a Tow 10 Tw a Hwŏ, 2 Hwŏ 1 Shih.
Another table runs —

10 Shu	equal to		1 Liu.
10 Liu	,, ,,		1 Chu.
24 Chu	,, ,,		1 Tael.
16 Taels	,, ,,		1 Catty.
2 Catties	,, ,,		1 Yin.
30 ,,	,, ,,		1 Kiun.
100 ,,	,, ,,		1 Pecul.
120 ,,	,, ,,		1 Shih or Stone
3 ,,	,, ,,		4 Pounds Avoirdupois.
84 ,,	,, ,,		1 Cwt.
1 Pecul	,, ,,		133⅓ Pounds Avoirdupois

4—Page 2—A *Le* is generally spoken of as
the third of a mile. Following are the usual—

Measures of Length,

Half a Tsun	equal to		1 Li.
5 Tsun	,, ,,		1 Fan.
5 Chih or Feet	,, ,,		1 Pú or Pace.
360 Pú	,, ,,		1 Lí or Mile.
250 Lí	,, ,,		1 Tú or Degree.
1 Degree	,, ,,		1460.44 Feet,

Gutzlaff says.—
The Le, or Chinese mile, contains 180 (each of ten feet) fa-
thoms, or Chang, equal to 1,897½ English feet, or 2,853 toises,
and 200 Le measure a degree of latitude. This measurement,
however, is not so well fixed as not to admit of doubt and varia-
tion. The missionaries divided the degree into 200 Le, each
Le amounting to 1,826 English feet, which gives the degree 69,
,166 English miles, or 11·131 French myriameters.
The land-measure is still less accurately defined : 5 Chih or
Covids make a Poo or Kung, and 63⅞ Mow one English acre—
in squares. 5 Chih—1 Poo,—140 Poo to one Mow, or 6,000
square covids.

5 ard 6—Page 5.—Statists differ as to the content of a Mow. Sir George Staunton estimated it at 1.000 square yards. At the Land office, Hongkong 1951$\frac{97}{100}$ were fixed as the standard. In Shanghae, Six mows and a sixtieth constitute an acre. The usual land measure table runs.—

5 *chih* 尺 make one 步 *pú* (pace), or 弓 *kung* (bow).

24 *pú* 步 make one 分 *fan* ;

60 *pú* 步 make one 角 *kioh* or horn ;

4 *kioh* 角 or 240 *pú* make one 畝 *mau*, or Chinese acre;

100 *mau* 畝 make one 頃 *k'ing*.

Taking the *chih* to be 12.587 inches, a square *pú* will measure 27.499636 square inches; this divided by 9, gives 3.0555 square yards; which multiplied by 240 *pú* gives 733.32 *sq. yds.* in a Chinese *mau*, equal to 6.61 *mau* to an English acre.

7—Page 5.—A good deal of erroneous statistic has been printed on this land tax point. The latest authority (Williams) says it ranges from 1½ to 10 cents a *mow*, or from 10 to 66 cents an acre, according to the quality of the land and difference of tillage. But there is a wide difference, it will be seen, between this and what is actually paid.

From Gutzlaff's "China opened," one of the best works extant, we take the following.—

LAND-TAX—TEEN-FOO.

The lands are divided into king and mow : 100 mow make a king ; 240 square poo make a mow ; and 5 chih, or covids, make a poo, (a chih is reckoned at 14⅝ inches.) Thus, 6$\frac{32}{7}$ Chinese mow make 1 English acre.

The grain is measured in the following manner :—6 suh make a kwei ; 10 kwei a chaou ; 10 chou a tsuy ; 10 tsuy a chö ; 10 chö a hö ; a shing, or 31⅔ cubic punts ; 10 shing a low, or 316 cubic punts; 5 tow o hwŏ, or 1580 cubic punts; and 2 hwŏ a shih, or 3160 cubic punts.

The whole arable area of China Proper, amounts to 7,875,149 king, 74 mow. Gardens, parks, and plantations 52,095 king. Lands and pastures in Mongolia, and Mantchouria, belonging to the eight standards, 80,248 king. This includes

		King.	mow.
lands belonging to the people paying taxes.		7,857,918	46
Imperial domains, lands belonging to the princes		13,838	
Do.	to the eight standards - -	140,128	71
Do.	to the Chinese military - - -	259,416	48
Do.	to the temples - - - -	8,620	
Do.	to the public institutions, and for the maintenance of poor scholars -	11,557	78
Shan-se lands, or mountain ridges - -		110	60
Arable soil in the Ele district, belonging to the eight standards - - - -		9,751	

From these lands the following revenue arises, 53,730,218 taels, viz.:—

		Taels.
Money sent to the capital	- - -	27,448,701
Do.	kept in the provincial treasury	7,561,677
Do.	kept in the district deposits	1,016,108
Do.	kept for exigencies	10,830,342
Commuted capitation tax	- - -	8,521,272
Rent for the lands of the eight standards	-	276,201
Do.	of the Chinese soldiers -	508,557
Rent from the lands belonging to the public institutions - - - - -		20,699
Expenses of transporting the money and grain to Peking - - - - - - -		2,339,661
For maintaining the aqeducts of Chih-le and Gan-hwuy - - - - -		212,000

The total amount of the land-tax, in kind, is 38,234,138 shih, viz.:—

		Shih.
Annual tribute sent to capital	- - -	2,561,278
Do.	sundries, insurance, additional contributions under various names -	891,397

For the use of the sailors on board the transports · · · · · ·	638,090
For the soldiers of the convoy ¯ · · ·	180,606
'Grain kept in stores of provincial granaries	33,792,880
Rent of eight standards' lands · · ·	200,244
Do. soldiers' land · · ·	373
Do. public institutions · · ·	19,760
	Taels.
Total amount of land-tax in specie · ·	53,730,218
Tax in kind, valued at 1½ tael, per shih ·	57,851,207
Sundry articles of tribute, as cotton, and silk piece–goods, metals, wax, &c, sent annually from the different provinces to Peking, and mostly bought for money arising from the land-tax · · · ·	2,316,632
TOTAL · · ·	113,898,057

In this calculation. however, it ought to be remembered, that we included the 33,792,330 shih of grain stored up in the provincial granaries, which does not belong exclusively to government, but is owned by the greater part of the people, and is only under the management of government officers.

In giving these sums, we have followed the statistics with great minuteness. In adding another 221,857 taels to the above sum, which arises from marshy land, it will be found that the sum total realized by the public from all the lands, is 113,619,914 taels.

For the satisfaction of the reader, we present this result of unwearied research also in details, in which, however, we have left out acres belonging to public bodies.

PROVINCES.	Inhabitants.	Square miles.	Inhabitants upon each square mile.	Commuted capitation tax	Lands paying taxes
					King. mow.
Chih-le - - -	27,990,871	58.949	473	424,444	227,256 50
Shan-tung - -	28,958,761	56,104	515	354,051	984,728 46
Shan-se - - -	14,004.210	55,268	253	642,006	532,854
Ho-nan -	23 037,171	65,104	354	120,268	718,208 64
Keang-soo -	37,843,501 }	92.961	774 }	250,764	447.546 27
Gan-hwuy	34,168.059			224 353	340,786 33
Keang-se - - -	30,426.999	72,176	421	183,145	462,187 27
Fokeen - - -	14,777.410	53,380,	276	180,499	128,626 64
Che-keang - -	26 256,784	39,150	671	237,518,	464,120 16
Hoo-pih - - -	27,370,098 }	144,770	317 }	109,999	594,439 44
Hoo-nan - -	18,652.507			77 036	313,024 73
Shen-se - -	10,207.256	154,008	164 }	240 313	258,404 12
Kan-suh - -	15,193,125 }			61,904	235,366 21
Sze-chuen -	21,435,678	166.800	128	56,991	463,819 39
Kwang-tung -	19,147 030	79,456	214	120,003	343,203 9
Kwang-se - - -	7,313,895	78,250	93	46,303	89,601 79
Yun-nan - -	5,561,32.	107.909	51	29 405	93,177 9
Kwei-shoo - -	5 288,219	64.554	82	137,801	268 54
Leaou-tung - -	942,003	Unknown.		23,474	115,240
	362,386,098	1,288 979		5,521 272	7,357 319 46

PROVINCES.	Regular land tax in silver.	Money sent to the capital.	Grain and seeds. Land tax in kind.	Grain sent to the capital.	Grain left in the provincial granaries.	Money remaining in the Provincial Treasurer's hands
	Taels.	Taels.	Shih.	Shih.	Shih.	Taels.
Chih-le	2,031,200	1 929,37	24 740		2 510,524	847,351
Shan-tung	3,260.000	3,001,36	507,680	83,258	2,959 386	553,802
Shan-se -	2 421 400	3 918,349	1 40,160	—	2,310 999	427.421
Honan -	3.139 000	2,991,35	248,86	9 25 1	2,310 999	378,480
Keang-soo -	3,207,200	1 314 49	378,050	1 015,917	1,520,000	1,276,998
Gan-hwuy	1,431,100	1,334,29	180,700	290,464	1,584,000	420,636
Keang se -	1 884,500	1 868 25	129,420	351.683	1,137,713	383,461
Fokeen	1,607,700	1,467,37	301,120	—	2,566,449	304,679
Che-keang -	2 556 900	2,205 31	383,100	621,473	2,900,020	310,642
Hoo-pih -	1,014.700	1,011,58	143 830	93,676	520,935	209,659
Hoo-nan -	1 085 700	1,033,03	144,450	95,540	702,133	277,130
Shen-se -	1.369,500	1,407,812	194,900	—	2,733,010	443,181
Kan suh -	219 200	2.025,025	484 090	—	3,280,009	101,909
Sze-chuen -	611,500	586 197	12,150	—	20,800	169,129
Kwang-tung	1,159 90.	990'470	341,720	—	2,953.661	245,121
Kwang-se - -	347,400	45 99	130,130	—	274,378	123,005
Yun-nan -	172,90	194,64	233,54	—	701,500	130,617
Kwei-choo -	107,800	70,809	123,270	—	507,000	39,074
Leaou-tung -	116,310	232,166	104.35	—	20,000	19,387
Total	28,306,400	27,448,701	5,193,738	2,561,279	33,792,330	7,561,677

Most of the provinces pay in a leap-year an additional sum both in money and kind. The payment upon each mow varies according to the quality of the land, from 1 to 400 cash.

The assessment having been made, the government not only levies that sum, but takes a certain per centage, as 5 to 10 per cent. insurance and loss in the carriage—for changing cash into silver, and vice versa—expenses of transportation, and many other items under diverse names. There is so great ingenuity shown in this affair, that the account is considerably swelled, and the peasant is obliged to pay at least from 20 to 30 per cent, above the assessment. Moreover, the extortions of the tax-gatherers, and the local mandarins, are far from trifling. Being badly paid, these officers are naturally very anxious to indemnify themselves upon the people. Hence arise bloody encounters, and the people show a most determinate resistance against the oppressors.

Many of the lands of the Mantchoo and Chinese soldiers are situated near the frontiers of the Meaou-taze territories. The greater part of the Ele area, has likewise been granted to these warriors. It is very natural that they should defend their own herd against their enemies, and thus become the natural bulwark of the adjacent districts.

Every collector must furnish a certain quantity both of money and grain. If he fails to do so, he must reimburse the deficit himself. His whole property is made surety for the due payment, and if this be insufficient, he is sent to an adjoining rich district, and permitted to exercise extortions, until he has obtained the requisite sum. Such a visit is feared by the people as much as the plague, many of the richer classes immediately abscond; whilst others hide their valuables.

It has often been remarked, that the immense populousness, and the taxes, which on an average are per mow 160 cash, and per king, 16 taels, (1 tael per English acre,) raise the price of grain higher than it values in other countries. Rice is not half so dear in Bengal as in China, Manilla is enabled to import large quantities to Macao, Java can furnish the market to advantage, and even in Japan it is much cheaper. We have nowhere found it to be at so low a price as at Canton, which is owing to the importation from foreign parts. The land is of very high value, and being parcelled out into many small portions, the cultivators are enabled to extract much more than a large landholder would be able to do. Thus it can pay heavier taxes, especially in the southern provinces; the soil yields a threefold, and often a fourfold harvest.

The richest province is Keang-soo, and it pays therefore an enormous tax; Chě-keang, the smallest province, is evidently over tax-

ed, whilst Sze-chuen, Yun-nan, Kwang-se, and Kwei-choo, pay
very little.

8.—Page 6. It is an axiom that in China
the institutions and practices of Government are
directly the reverse of those in Europe. In the
administration of justice this is illustrated ; and,
proud as we are of our forms of trial in the abstract,
there is room for believing that benefit would ac-
crue were we to borrow somewhat from the mode of
Chinese procedure. A writer in the Chinese Repository for September 1833, says.—

" Justice is often administered in the most sum-
" mary manner. Not unfrequently, in minor cases,
" the man receives the punishment and again goes
" free the same hour in which he commits the crime.

" The forms of trial are simple. There is no jury,
" no pleading. The criminal kneels before the ma-
" gistrate, who hears the witnesses and passes sen-
" tence ; he is then remanded to prison or sent to
" the place of execution. Seldom is he acquitted."

This non-acquittal arises in the majority of cases
from the circumstance of all the facts being elicited by the Elders, (who, in reality, are both Grand
and Petty Jury) before the criminal is remitted to
the *Yuen.* The writer goes on to say —

" When witnesses are wanting, he is sometimes
" tortured until he gives in evidence against him-
" self."

This atrocity, we have reason to believe, is found
to occur in district cities principally—Police Magis-
trates in cities relieving Elders of their customary
patriarchal duties. These Stipendiaries, no doubt,
are very severe in their mode of eliciting truth.

Illustrative of the difference in magisterial proceedings, is the course pursued at Hongkong, where,
until very recently, examinations in chief were con-

ducted by unlettered and inexperienced Police In-
spectors;—the wonder being, not that Justice was
so administered, as that so much, with the in-
struments, was effected. But, from the Police
office to the Police-Court, and from that to the
Supreme tribunal, it would be interesting to ascer-
tain, from actual statistic, what proportion of the
whole number of charges meet a decree. In the
Supreme Court, though the juries are by no means
fastidious with Chinese culprits, the number of
cases resulting in convictions, is, certainly, under
the half of the total sent up.

9—Page 14.—This calculation of £12 per ton
is made on the estimate of 1250 cash for a Shanghae dollar, or tael weight of silver. A worse exchange, say 1000 Cash only, would make the price
of the iron in pigs on a par with English rod, obtainable in Hongkong, as we write this note (February 1858.) almost a year after the remark to
which it refers was made, at $3,75 per pecul, which,
at an exchange on England of 4s. 9d, would be
nearly £15 per ton. When to this we add the fact
that Pig iron averages only £4 per ton at a Shipping port * it will be seen, that so far as Iron goes,
China's sand cannot compete with England's ore.

[After writing this, we obtained the opinion
of an experienced iron worker (Mr Dick of Hong-

---

* The price of iron has been subject to great fluctuations,—
especially of late years. In September 1824, the current price
of common bars at the shipping port was £9 a-ton ; in March
1825, a period of great speculation, it rose to £14 ; but by March
1830, owing to the extended production consequent on this high
rate, it fell to £3,,5s. a-ton. Since that period, in consequence of
the increased demand for railways and other purposes, the price
has risen considerably, and at present (February 1842) it is quoted, in bars, at £6 15s. a-ton ; that of pig being £4. Taking the
quantity stated above, 1,500,000 tons, as the present annual pro-

kong) on a sample which we brought from one
of the foundries. This opinion runs as follows—"The
pig of four pounds weight, which you tell me is just
as it ran from the furnace, may not be classed with
common English pig.   At one heat it drew out in
five eighths-bar, an inch wide, to the length of seventeen inches, and is so malleable and tenacious that
my men wished to make some "nuts" from it ;—
articles for which we always use the very best material.   I should class it with the best Swedish, and
if the Chinese only possessed rolling machines, it
might be sold for bar of quality not inferior to Iron
for which I am now paying here, landed from England, £14 per ton "]—

10.—Page 15.—The quantity of Silk used by
each woman in binding the horn cannot be less than
half a pound.   Produced from their own cocoons,
the cost will be trifling; but the appearance of such
an exuberance of silk cord could not fail in inducing a reflection on the use of an article which,
since trade has been released from the fetters that
bound it prior to the war of 1840, has had so
much to do with the currency and exchange of
England and the whole mercantile world.   Prior to
1841 the total quantity of Silk exported from China
did not exceed 3,000 bales a year—Fifteen times
three thousand is now the average;—and for the
year 1856–7 the deliveries of China Silk in England, alone, amounted to 74,215 bales.

From enquiries made we find that this extraor-

---

duce, and applying this last price of £4, gives the value in pig at
£6,000,000 ; to which, adding £3,000,000 as the cost of convert-
ing seven-tenths thereof (the common estimate) into bars, bolts,
rods, sheets, and the other forms of wrought iron, makes the annual value of the manufacture £9,000,000.— *Waterston's Cy-
clopædia.*

dinary difference in export is not effected on increase
of produc tion so much as on the inability, (for
want of means,) or the carelessness of the Chinese
to indulge in the luxury, either as *tsien* for the
tail, bands for the waist, or other form of indulgence; and our ruminations have led us to make
the following calculation. Allowing the population
of China to be 300 millions (doubtful,—*See Note on
population*) and that each man, woman, and child
uses a quarter of a pound of silk cord a year for a
plait to the end of the tail (a quarter of a pound, be
it remembered, being a minimum quantity,—some
of the richer classes plaiting in several new *tsien* in
the course of a year, these again using half a
pound, and even a pound at a time) we find that
the total quantity used, 75 millions of pounds,
equals the weight of 750,000 bales. Estimating
the price again at four pounds for a Sovereign, we
have, in the shape of a tax to carry out a whim
imposed by the Tartars on their subjugation of
the country, a total sum of nearly Nineteen millions of pounds Sterling per annum—not far short
of the interest on the debt created by our fore-
fathers in England to carry on the wars

Whilst on the subject of China-men's tails, we
may remark that the region in which we found
the peculiar head dress educing this note is that
in which the natives exhibited for a lengthen-
ed period the firmest determination not to submit
to the degradation of a tail ; and that this feeling
still rankles in the minds of the people was clear
from the questions of several of them. Being taken
for rebels in disguise, as a feeler, one said—" Why
do you not wear a tail?" (the rebels have discarded
it)—*Answer* " Because it is not the custom in our
western country—Why do you?—"*Answer, (an-*

grily)—Because the Tatsing dynasty insist-on it !"

Martini, a Roman Catholic priest of the Seventeenth century, in his narrative of the Manchou conquest, thus writes on this opposition of the people to wearing a Queu.—

" While the Tartars, A. D. 1644, were over running the Provinces on the North of the Yellow River, the Chinese prepared to make a stand in the South. They proclaimed at Nanking-Hungkwang a descendant of the Mings ; but another pretender made his appearance, and while the rivals were discussing their claims, the Tartar hordes were pouring down from the North. They met with little opposition until they appeared before the famous and opulent city of Yangchow. Seu, a faithful minister of Hungchow defended the place with a large garrison ; but he was at length forced to yield. The Tartars pillaged every dwelling, slaughtered the whole population, both citizens and soldiers * ; and lest their putrifying remains should breed pestilence, collected them into houses, and reduced the city and suburbs to ashes. When they advanced against Nanking, the General Hwangchang met them on the opposite bank of the river and proved that Tartars might be beaten by Chinese. But he fell pierced by the arrow of a treacherous subordinate, and with him perished the hope of his country. His soldiers fled in confusion. The Emperor betook himself to flight ; and the same wretch who had slain the general, now betrayed his prince into the hands of the enemy. The unhappy monarch was sent to Peking and strangled. Thus obtaining easy possession of the Southern capital, the Tartars extirpated the family of Hung kwang, and marched against Hangchow. At that famous metropolis, prince Lo of the Imperial blood had assumed the sceptre. But, as if in apprehension of a speedy fall, he declined the Imperial title ; and in fact he had worn the crown only three days (scarcely as long as the kings in Chinese comedies) when the Tartars arrived. *   *   *   *   *   *   *

Crossing the Tsien'tang they took possession of Shaouhing, and the rest of Chehkiang submitted without resistance. When however they required the Chinese to shave their heads *a la Manchou*, both soldiers and people began to sharpen their weapons ; rather solicitous for their jetty locks then for their country. Risking their heads to save their hair, they fought bravely, ex-

---

* When the rebels took Nanking, in 1853, in making that loudly decried extermination of the Tartars they only, retaliated, it will be seen... "root and branch "—blood for blood.

pelled the enemy from Shaouhing, obliged him to recross the
Tsient'ang, and if they had followed up these successes they
might have cleared the province of invaders. But, as if satisfied
with having averted the razor from their heads, they paused and
fortified the Southern bank. The Tartars were thus held at
bay for a whole year. — *Translated from the Latin of Martini, by
the Revd W. A. P. Martin.*

12 at Pages 21 and 22.—*Tah-yeong-pow-tea*
signifies "Precious temple of the Great and Brave"

Sam-sing-cheng-veh. "The holy footsteps of
the three lived (Buddh.)"—

Seaou-yun-laou—" The peaceful departments."

Me-leh-tong-tien—" Me-leh (the name of the
Buddh) comprehending the heavens."—

11.—Page 21—Though their accounts of the
idol's creation are confused and inconsistent, the
priests furnish travellers with a native memoir of
which the following is a translation.—

THE STONE IMAGE OF BUDDH. *The measurement of the great Buddh of the stone city mountain in Yok-chow, as reported by a priest. —*

Thirty *lê* east of *Sui-kê*, in the district of *Sing-
chong*, there is a Stone city, called the Secreted
Mountain. In reality it is the Western entrance
of a defile called *Teen-toey*, and is distant five or
six *lê* from the capital of the district—near the
peak of the twin mountains. The image is chisel-
led out of a rock so perfectly that it is without
seam or crevice in which grass or shrub can grow.
Nor is there any hole or cave into which Tiger or
wolf can enter. To external appearance, the place
is like a beautiful hall ;—and, with deep set eyes,
Buddh sits in a really god-like place. Truly the
maker must have had a special design in this matter. Right and left—before and behind—this temple is surrounded by rocks;—on all sides they stand
as attendant servants.

According to the ancient records of *Low-tsz,*
in the fourth year of *Wang-ming,*—*Fow-to,* whose
name was *Cheng-oo,* reverently vowed by the three
lives of Buddha that he would make the image of
Me-leh,—the name of one of these gods; and in the
second month of the twelfth year of *Tien-cam,* of the
Leong Dynasty, he made a commencement with
his chisel—laying out the divine abode,—110 chak
(Chinese feet) high,—70 broad and 50 deep. The
body of his Buddhistic majesty was to be 100 *chak*
high, seated upon a throne 56 *chak* broad. His
face from the commencement of the hair on the
forehead to the chin was 18 *chak,*—about 22 *chak*
long, and broad in proportion.

His eyes were 6 feet 3 inches long, his eye brows
7 feet 5 inches, his ears 12 feet, and his nose 5 feet 3
inches, his mouth 6 feet 2 inches.—From where
his hair commenced to the top of his head, was 13
feet; his fingers and palm were 12 feet 5 inches
long,—broad 6 feet 5 inches;—his feet were of like
measurement ;—his knees spread apart 45 feet,
and the whole figure was beautiful and dignified,
resembling a living being of the age of thirty two
years. It was altogether most complete.

In the fifth year of *Ham Peng,*—*Tuen-tung*
made a journey to *Teen-toey,* and as his way lay by
the Mountain he ventured on an inspection of this
wonderful image of such extraordinary dimensions.
The sight of it induced profound reflection. Beside
this image, which is in the district of *Ka-seng-peng,*
under the whole heavens there can be no other to
equal it.* Therefore he determined to engrave the
idol's dimensions on a stone, in order to preserve a

---

* Were the dimensions given in this memoir correct, which
they are not—the image, large as it is, would be under the proportions of the old Colossus of Rhodes.

memorial for spectators from every quarter;—so
gratifying the eyes and ears with information regarding it. Extraordinary is thy influence, Oh
Divine Spirit!—Extraordinary the workmanship
on thy exterior ;—and, as long as generations
endure, so long will thy fame, and that of Low,
who carved thee, be told in glowing language.

This matter was recorded in the year 王 寅
*Yum-yun, in the reign of Kampeng of the Sung
Dynasty ;—and Teo-hung, other wise Pak
Cheong, desirous of propagating intelligence,
prepared this document in the 31st year of the
9th month of the reign of Taoukwang of the Ta
tsing Dynasty ;—the head Priest here, with one
of his co-adjutors, setting up the tablet on which
it is imprinted.*

Second 11.—Page 35.—It is is the custom in
the south of China to call a person by the name
attached to the family name; and in Canton, *Woo,*
or *Ahwoo,* would be the cognomen of the hospitable
individual now written of. At *Fong-je-how,* however, and in the north generally, the chief, or family
name is used with an affix, by way of politeness, of
Seen-sang (Scholar) and this term of *Seen-sang,*
(educated man,) is applied honararily even to those
who have no education to boast of. *Luh* Seen-
sang, then, as we call him (the head of the *Wan-
ho* firm,) is, it is believed, a fair specimen of
" Young China." Impatient at having to do business
at Shanghae through the native broker *Coong-
ming,* he has commenced the study of the English
language, in which, in a short time, he promises to
become a proficient. Once able to speak fluently,
he then intends trading direct with the foreign
merchant.

Second 12. at Page 37.—If the reader at this point will retrace what is written, he will find that, in a working week's travel of 424 *lé* (or after the average of 70 *lé* per diem, quite as much as can be done with comfort) we passed through 73 villages and two walled Cities; and that of the villages we have noted upwards of 21,000 families, or at the rate of 5 souls to a family, over 105,000 people. The number of in habitants at the walled cities mentioned we are not in a position to give; but it may be of interest to the curious in such matters to observe that, for the villages and distance given, the rate of population is about 750 per running mile. For running mile may be read square mile; but this may not be taken as the rate for the province, because, of plain where people reside, to mountain where they do not reside, the proportion is as one to three; that is to say, the mountain covers three parts, and the plain one, of the districts traversed. This is an under estimate, and one of plain to five of mountain would be nearer the mark. Though, therefore, the population of the district cities may tend to swell the aggregate in a very great degree, there appears grave reason for doubting whether the published statement of the census of 1812, * giving 670 souls for every square mile of the province of Chekiang is not an over estimate;—and that there is reason to believe that the populations of the most populous districts have formed the bases for estimating that · · · · · ·

---

* Indeed the estimate made by De Guignes in 1743 and by Allerstein a score of years later, of 15½ millions for the whole province, is much more likely to approximate with the real number than the census of 1812 (25¼ millions) as given by Gutzlaff in his tables quoted at 98 *supra*, and cited by other savans without a moment's reflection, apparently, on the probability of the correctness.

the whole number of inhabitants is so great as twenty six and a half millions.

[The writer regrets his inability to furnish the Chinese characters promised on page 1.—The M. S. of them, besides some lithographed plates and other papers, of which use would have been made in this publication, were lost during the Vandal-like proceedings of the Hongkong Government for what was deemed a libel on its Lieutenant Governor in 1859.]

[The following letter gives a concise abstract of the foregoing Notes of travel.]

SHANGHAE, 17*th April*, 1857.

To the Editor of the NORTH-CHINA HERALD.

DEAR SIR,—The following brief particulars of a journey from Ningpo, *viâ Teen muh san,* and the Confucian Pass in *Anwhuy* Province, to this place may be interesting to your local readers.

We (Dr. Macgowan and myself) left Ningpo in a boat on the night of the 24th ult., and early the following morning reached *Kongkêaou,* a small village in a southerly and westerly direction, some 60 or 70 *le* from Ningpo, where we took to the chairs carried with us, and proceeded by the way of the Heaven Struck Rock and *Ningkong jow* to *Haoulung,* where we slept in an Ancestral Hall. That day we travelled, somewhat circuitously, 93 *le*—though the course and distance made good was only 7 miles N. and 7 miles W.

March 26*th*—From *Haoulung* to *Hô pé chee,* where we again slept in an Ancestral Hall.—Distance travelled 100 *le.*—Course good, S. 27 miles—W. 12.

March 27*th*—From *Hô pé chee* to the *Poosan* monastery.—Distance travelled 86 *le.*—Course good, S. 13 miles—W. 18.

March 28*th*—From the *Poosan* monastery, by the way of the Iron washing Beds and Smelteries, to the *hien* city of *Singchong*—taking up our quarters at the *Tow va sze,* or Temple of the Great Buddha, a demi idol 51 feet high from its seat, cut out of the solid rock. Distance travelled 87 *le.*—Course good, S. 1 mile—W. 11 miles.

March 29*th*—Sunday,—kept as a day of rest.

March 30*th*—Travelled half a day to the district city of *Dzing,* where we slept at a monastery out side. Distance 40 *le.*—Course good, N. 5½ miles—W. 7.

March 31*st*—Through a very mountainous country to *Shihchong*, a hamlet in a dell, where we slept in a house by a paper manufactory. Distance 90 *le.*—Course, N. 11 miles—W. 21.

April 1*st*—To *Foong je how*, where we were met by, and pressed to pass the night at the residence of a Tea maker and merchant of the family name of *Luh.* · Distance travelled (more than half a-day along the sides of mountains) 67 *le.*—Course N. 14¼ miles—W. 25.

April 2*nd*—A short walking distance north of *Foong-je-how* we took boat at noon, and at mid-night entered the River *Tsien Tang.* Estimated course good, 20 miles west.

April 3*rd*—About 11 A. M. reached the *hien* city of *Foo-yang*, never before passed through by Europeans. Pass through, and at night reached a monastery among the hills, called *Ka-yuen-sze*, where we slept. Water travelling estimated at 110 *le*—Land 45 *le.* Computed course to *Foo-yang*, S. 6 miles—W. 29.—*Foo-yang* to *Ka-yuen-sze*, N. 13 miles —W. 5.

April 4*th*—Passed through the *hien* city of *Linghaen* (not visited before by Europeans) and at night reached the Monastery or Caravansara of *Vok-hing*, where we slept. Distance travelled 90 *le.*—Course good N. 10 miles—W. 21¼.

April 5*th*—Kept as the Sabbath—no travelling.

April 6*th*—This day reached the *Chaou-ming* monastery, nearly at the top of the Eastern *Teen muh san*, never before visited by Foreigners. Here we slept. Distance travelled, two-thirds in ascent, 45 *le.* Course good N. 7½ miles—W. 6.

April 7*th*—Travelling, part of the day, from the Eastern *Teen muh* to the *Choey yen sze*, or monastery, an establishment covering, within walls, 5½ acres of ground, at the southern foot of the Western *Teen muh.* Distance travelled 24 *le.* – Course good, S. 2¼ miles.– W. 6½.

April 8*th*—Half a-day on foot to the monastery on the Eastern. *Teen muh*, and afterwards to the top of the mountain and back. Total distance about 32 *le.* Course of our journey good, N. 3¾ miles—W. 1¼.

April 9*th*—Passed into *Anwhuy*, and that night slept in a Tavern in the village of *Toong haeu.* This was the most western point reached. Distance travelled 60 *le.* Course good, N. 7¾ miles—W. 13¾.

April 10*th*—By the way of the Confucian Pass into Chekiang Province again, through the *hien* city of *Gnan keih* (locally called *Aan-* " strike one of its people on the Emperor's high way? Were it not for " our regard to the foreigners you accompany, we would take you all to " the nearest authority, and there get you a hearty bambooing " I mention this circumstance the tone of the admonition implying more

cheh) and on to the *hien* city of *Haou-fung* (or *Shaou-foong*) where we slept at the *Kwanti mew* (Temple) out side. Distance travelled 74 *le.* – Course good, N. 11¼ miles—E. 22.

April 11*th*—From Haoufung to the *Maichee* Ferry,—three miles beyond the town, where we took boat at 8 P. M. and a little before midnight started for Hoochow, which was reached at 11 of the following day. There we remained till Monday morning, the Doctor then leaving me by boat for *Kan Poo*, on his return to Ningpo. From *Haou-fung* to *Maichee* Ferry the distance travelled was 85 *le*. Course good N. 17 miles—E. 20.

While in the boats, four days from Hoochow to Shanghae, sometimes sailing at 5 or 6 knots an hour, tugging at 5, or skulling at 2 knots— latterly through a continued series of winding creeks, it was not possible to fix the courses and distance with anything like correctness, and I have therefore not attempted it. *

As it is my intention to publish fuller particulars in the shape of a hand book to the whole land travel, two-thirds of which was through districts never before traversed by Europeans in their usual costume, at all events during the remembrance of "the oldest inhabitant," we found the people as kind as it is possible to conceive. A nod or a smile was instantly returned, and a salute promptly responded to in a spirit indicating respect and appreciation of the compliment. Certainly, if prejudice does exist against foreigners in these regions, it was not exhibited towards us ; and there appears to me no reason to doubt but similar excursions could be extended in perfect safety to the most western parts of the empire.

If I might judge from a little incident in the district of Ningkwoh (Auwhuy) where one of our bearers struck the native guide for leading us over a tiresome path, I should say but little sympathy exists between the people of the several provinces. Complaint being made by the guide to one of his countrymen who came up with us on their return from a pilgrimage to the Eastern *Teen-muh*, the words used by them were—"How dare you, *Chekiang* men, to come into our province, and than is here expressed, because I think it tends to show that with our quarrel with the Cantonese the people of other provinces will not care a jot ;—and that unless the Chinese Government initiate it, (their means being required for the attempt to subdue a rebellion in which, *in spirit*, all participate) the war need not, of necessity, be

---

* My companion having remarked at starting that the latitudes and longitudes of the different cities in our route were variously stated by different authorities, I was particular in noting our course with all the pains in my powers, so as to check to half a degree at least. The rate of walking was fixing at an average to ten *le* [a little over 3 miles] per hour.—W. T.

extended north of its present field. News travels so slowly in the in: terior that fifty miles from Ningpo the mass of the people never heard that that place was in the hands of the English for some time in 1841 and 42; and unless brought more closely to their senses than is now apparent, the present generation of people away from the Northern Consular cities may never hear of the "Second War with China."—I am, Dear Sir, your's truly.

WILLIAM TARRANT.

P. S.—Throughout the whole journey I did not see, beyond a few well worn cloth winter Jackets, a solitary yard of foreign fabric. I did not see an offensive weapon of any kind, sword, spear or firelock;—and none but small footed women crossed our path.—W. T.

The appended wood cut gives an approximation to the tracks out and home. As stated above, the distance and course from Fong-je-how, by the Canal and River Tsien-tang to Fu-yang, had to be guessed at; and the following latitudes and longitudes of the cities visited, as found in the Chinese Repository for 1844, do not coincide with the places laid down on the Southern line.

Sing-chong hien 昌新 in *Shou-hing-fu.* Lat. 29.32,—Long 120, 50.

Dzing 山東 or *Shing-hien* in *Shou-hing-fu.* Lat. 29.36—Long 120, 42, 47.

Fu-yang hien 富陽 in *Hang-chow-fu.** Lat. 30.04, 47,—Long 119, 55, 37.

Ling-ngan hien 臨安 in *Hang-chow-fu.* Lat. 30.16,—Long 119, 42.

Ngan-kih hien 安吉 in *Hu-chow-fu.* Lat. 30.40—Long 119, 36.

Hiau-fung hien 孝豐 in *Hu-chow-fu.* Lat. 30.30—Long 119, 36.

Hoo-chow-fu 湖州 Departmental city.* Lat. 30.52, 48—Long 119, 52, 54.

---

* According to French observations.

ERRATUM.—In the Index to Order of Travel, for Department of Hoo-chow in " Kiang-su " read in " Che-kiang."

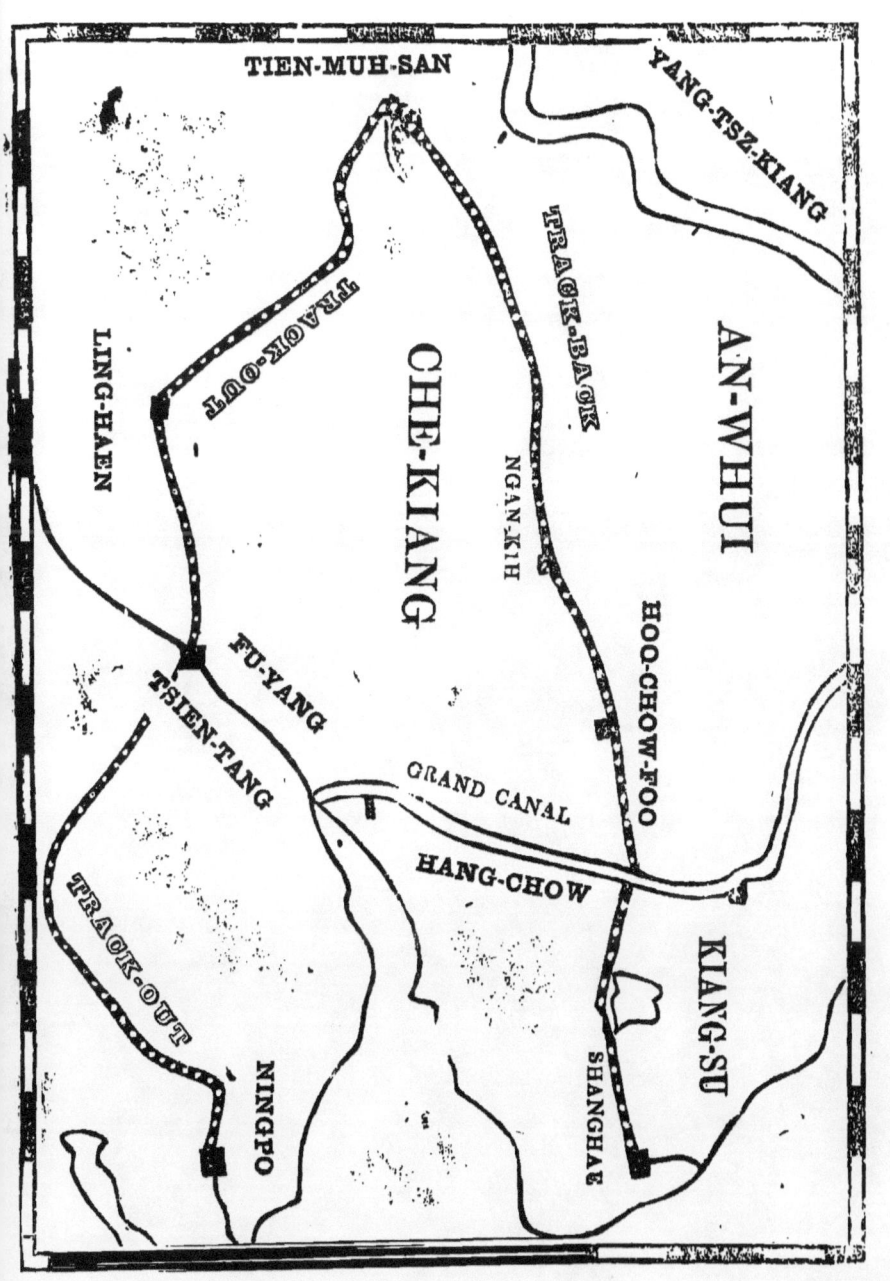

www.ingramcontent.com/pod-product-compliance
Lightning Source LLC
Chambersburg PA
CBHW020758020726
47495CB00008B/2490